# It's a Weird Winter Wonderland

# It's a Weird Winter Wonderland

Edited by Robert Bose
and Axel Howerton

COFFIN HOP PRESS LTD / CANADA

**It's a Weird Winter Wonderland**

First Edition:
Various; Edited by Robert Bose/Axel Howerton

Copyright © 2017 Coffin Hop Press Ltd.

All rights reserved.

No part of this text may be reproduced, distributed or transmitted in any form or by any means, including photocopying, recording, or other electronic or mechanical methods, without the prior written permission of the publisher, except in the case of brief quotations embodied in critical reviews and certain other noncommercial uses as permitted by Canadian copyright law.

For permission requests and other concerns:

Coffin Hop Press Ltd.
200 Rivervalley Crescent SE
Calgary, Alberta Canada  T2C 3K8
www.coffinhop.com
info@coffinhop.com

Publisher's Note: This is a work of fiction. Names, characters, places, and incidents are a product of the author's imagination or are used fictitiously. Any resemblance to actual persons, living or dead; businesses, companies, events, or locales is entirely coincidental.

Book design © 2017  Coffin Hop Press Ltd

*Wreckless Eyeballing* © 2017 - David James Keaton

*That's A Wrap* © 2017 – Will Viharo

*Riven* © 2017 – Sarah L. Johnson

*Up The Chimney* © 2017 – Steve Brewer

*Ho Ho Ho* © 2017 – Brent Nichols

*Of Gathering Gloom*© 2017 – Jessica McHugh

*A Vampire, A Burglar, and a Hippie...* © 2017 – Scott S. Phillips

*Saint Nikki"s Revenge* © 2017 – Laurie Zottman


ISBN 978-0-9947378-6-1

*For all the weirdoes
who love the holidays.*

*Keep it dark, keep it weird,*

*Keep it festive.*

# Contents

| | |
|---|---|
| **FOREWORD** | 1 |
| **UP THE CHIMNEY** STEVE BREWER | 7 |
| **WRECKLESS EYEBALLING** DAVID JAMES KEATON | 33 |
| **SAINT NIKKI'S REVENGE** LAURIE ZOTTMANN | 45 |
| **THAT'S A WRAP** WILL VIHARO | 77 |
| **A VAMPIRE, A BURGLAR, AND AN AGING HIPPIE WALK INTO A MALL** SCOTT S. PHILLIPS | 103 |
| **RIVEN** SARAH L. JOHNSON | 135 |
| **HO HO HO** BRENT NICHOLS | 155 |
| **OF GATHERING GLOOM** JESSICA MCHUGH | 193 |
| **LINER NOTES** | 249 |
| **ABOUT THE AUTHORS** | 261 |

# Foreword

## Winter is weird.

It really is.

Dark, and cold, and full of terrors...

I mean, holidays. Full of *holidays*.

Seriously though, look at *Xmas*, or *Christmas*, or *Solstice,* or what-have-you. Some people swear by their ancient book that Christmas is a sacred birthday party celebrating the Son-of-a-God that they worship (at least that once a year), and on the other hand, it's a well-documented throwback to a variety of Norse/Celtic/Pagan-mostly Viking traditions involving the winter solstice, inside-trees, and a whole lot of drinking – as Vikings are wont to do. Over time these two concepts smashed together, fluidly attracting cultural enhancements from across the world, from Santa (and his Evil-Spock-version, Krampus) to flying reindeers – with, and without optional night-light nose GPS; trees dolled up like fifties burlesque dancehall queens, draped in tinsel and lit up with electric sex appeal (No! *You* have a fetish!); Feasts of Yule, cakes of fruit, cookies of ginger... Sounds like a hell of a shopping list.

## IT'S A WEIRD WINTER WONDERLAND

And it ain't just Xmas anymore, is it? We kick it off with Thanksgiving (all the way back in October, if you're Canadian); *Chanukah (Hanukkah? Channukkah? Xanuka?* However you spell it, it's kind of the celebration of the never-ending candle...); *Eid Al Adha; Kwanzaa;* Slackernalia; Kerabotsmas (if'n you're Dudely like that); various New Years; the ol' office Secret Santa/pantsless booze-pocalypse; and, of course, a Festivus for the rest of us...

Inevitably, this means that this high holiday season means something a little different to everyone. Everyone has their own folklore, their own traditions, their own family and personal stories. Sometimes it's about your drunk uncle pissing in the punch bowl; sometimes it's about cloven hooves on rooftops. Maybe it's Santa, or maybe it's not...

There's something about "The Most Wonderful Time of the Year" that brings out the best, and the worst, in our imaginations and our storytelling. While holiday tales can tend to run towards the sickly-sweet and family-friendly, for every *Miracle on 34th Street*, there's a *Bad Santa*; for every *'Twas The Night before Christmas*, there's an *Ice Harvest*.

Ever see the movie *Trading Places*? Dan Ackroyd is riding the city bus, decked out in a filthy Santa suit, he pulls a whole goddamn smoked salmon out from under his shirt and chomps down on it, getting an equal

# IT'S A WEIRD WINTER WONDERLAND

amount of cheese-and-vomit encrusted fake beard. He gets off the bus and a dog pisses on his leg, it begins to rain, and his attempt to shoot himself in the head fails. That's a certified holiday classic, right there. Just like:

Ol' Ebenezer redeeming his filthy, greedy soul.

That beautiful old Bailey Savings and Loan.

Melchior and Gaspar and Baltasar and Charlie fucking Brown.

Little Ralphie running his hand up the sexiest damn lamp in all of creation.

Those silly newlyweds and their Gifts of the Magi.

Bing and Danny and Fred and Rosemary and Irving bloody Berlin.

Frank Costanza declaring "I got a lotta problems with you people!"

As holidays go, this is our favourite time of year.

A whole month of booze, debauchery, overeating and presents.

In the spirit of Clark W. Griswold, we wanted to make you something special this year. Just a little something from us at Coffin Hop Press to you, nestled all snug in your beds, with visions of John McClane blasting uzi's echoing in your heads. So, we called up some pals – some amazingly talented, and generally gonzo writer-types, and we said, "Let it snow, motherfuckers!"

## IT'S A WEIRD WINTER WONDERLAND

And, lo' you hold the beauteous results in your hot little mittens.

Seven sweet short stories, flavoured with hot buttered rum, cinnamon, spice and whiskey galore! And a twisted eggnog-scented novella in a blazing inferno of a pear tree.

We hope it enhances your holiday spirit.

*Eid Mubarak!*

*Chag Urim Sameach!*

*Habari Gani!*

Happy holidays!

And Merry Christmas, you filthy animals.


Robert Bose and Axel Howerton

Editors-in-Crime

Coffin Hop Press

Calgary, Alberta

October 17, 2017

# Up the Chimney
## Steve Brewer

The way Muriel snapped awake, she knew there must've been a noise in the house. She lay perfectly still, listening for footfalls or the creak of the hardwood floors.

She and George had confronted their share of trespassers over the years. Bums, mostly, or drunken teens set on partying at the white farmhouse at the end of the long, gravel road. George usually ran them off by brandishing the old Colt revolver he kept in the drawer of the bedside table. The sight of the cowboy pistol with its eight-inch barrel was such a powerful persuader, he'd never had to pull the trigger.

Muriel sat up, wincing at the squeak of the bedsprings. She listened hard. Nothing for a moment, then – there! – a faint voice. A man's voice.

Her breath caught in her throat. No men at Muriel's house, not anymore. Their two boys had grown up and moved into town years ago. George died last year, out in the cornfield, felled by a stroke so sudden and brutal, it was as if he'd been struck down by the Hand of God.

She checked her glowing alarm clock. 11:22 p.m. Her eyeglasses were next to the clock, and she slipped them on in the dark, as if they would help her hear better.

There it was again. She couldn't make out what the man was saying. So faint, so far away. Muriel strained her ears, listening. The noise seemed to be coming from downstairs.

Had she left the television on? She'd done that a few times lately, stumbling downstairs at dawn to find some inane morning show chattering away. She knew such forgetfulness was a sign of mental decline. She'd told no one, of course. She was nearly eighty years old, and her sons kept insisting that she move into town to live in one of those homes for old folks.

To hell with that. Muriel had lived on this thousand-acre farm her whole life, first with her parents, then with George, working the land, raising livestock, saving and scraping, making the most of things. She planned to die right here.

But not tonight. Not on Christmas Eve.

Her sons and their wives and her five grandkids were scheduled to arrive in the morning for Christmas Day celebrations. She thought about the gilt-wrapped gifts stacked around her tree downstairs. Had they attracted a thief? The notion infuriated her. She didn't know how many Christmases she had left, and she wouldn't let a burglar ruin this one.

Muriel slid open the drawer of the bedside table, working by feel in the dark, and lifted out the old revolver without making a sound. The heavy gun was a comfort in her hands.

The voice again. Just one word. Not much more than a whisper in her ear, but she could've sworn it said, "Help!"

What in God's name was going on downstairs?

Keeping the pistol pointed at the ceiling, Muriel threw back the covers and swung her feet to the floor. Her soft slippers were right where she'd left them, and her feet slid into them automatically. She stood, her white flannel nightgown unfurling around her skinny legs until the hem reached the floor. It was chilly in the house. She wanted to put on her robe to cover her bare arms, but that would mean setting down the Colt, and she didn't want to risk the noise.

She slipped across the bedroom to the open door and paused to listen.

Definitely a man's voice, but muffled, as if he were shut in a closet. The same word over and over – "Help!"

"Oh, my," she whispered.

The call for help could be a ploy, a way to lure her downstairs. Muriel held the Colt before her in both hands as she moved to the top of the stairs where she could see the closed front door and the empty foyer. Moonlight spilled across the floor from the front windows, illuminating the worn rugs she'd braided from flour sacks so long ago, back when she and George couldn't afford better.

After his death last year, her sons had hired a locksmith to install new deadbolts on the doors and alarms on the windows. If she insisted on living alone out here in the "boonies," they'd said, she should have the best security money could buy.

She could see three unblinking green lights on the white control panel by the front door, meaning the burglar alarm was set and hadn't been tripped. Nobody had come in the windows or doors. Muriel eased down the stairs, keeping close

# UP THE CHIMNEY

## STEVE BREWER

to the wall so the wooden steps wouldn't creak. No sign of movement downstairs. Just that muffled, strangled voice.

When she reached the bottom of the stairs, she could tell the voice was coming from the living room. Muriel crept across the foyer and peeked in, seeing nothing unusual. The TV was dark. The familiar furniture sat in its usual places. She could even make out the boxy shapes of the gifts stacked around the fresh pine tree she'd spent all day decorating. That was a relief. How would she have explained to the grandkids that Santa's gifts had been stolen—

"Help!"

She wheeled to her left, cocking back the hammer of the pistol with her thumb. The *click* seemed very loud in the still house.

"Help me! Please!"

The voice was coming from the fireplace.

Gun at the ready, Muriel flicked on the overhead light. She could tell at a glance the room was unoccupied, and the fieldstone fireplace contained nothing but the ashes and charred logs from yesterday's fire.

"Help!"

The voice was coming from *inside* the fireplace. From up in the chimney.

# IT'S A WEIRD WINTER WONDERLAND

The first image that flashed into her mind was Santa Claus, sliding down a chimney in his red-and-white costume while his reindeer stamped and snorted on the roof. Such childish nonsense, it made her chuckle at her own foolishness. She might be slipping, but not so much that she believed in visits from Santa.

No, some man, some *thief*, had tried to come down her chimney, aiming to steal her Christmas gifts. And now he was stuck in there.

Muriel had heard of such things on the TV news, idiots who thought chimneys were straight chutes inside, an easy way to get into a house. Muriel knew better. She understood about drafts and angles, the way the interior of the flue narrowed to make sure the smoke went up, instead of flooding into the room. A *child* couldn't slither into the house that way, much less a grown man.

"Help!"

Muriel tiptoed across the room and leaned over, trying to look up the flue. Nothing but darkness.

"Please help me."

The man sounded desperate, breathless, in pain.

Muriel eased the hammer down on the pistol, no sense going around with a cocked gun when she clearly didn't need it. She might shoot her own foot off. She set the Colt on an end table next to her plaid sofa, only a step or two away from the hearth.

She leaned over to the fireplace again, beneath the five red stockings embroidered with the names of her grandkids, and called, "Hello?"

A pause, then the man in the chimney said, "Oh, thank God." His voice cracked, as if he were on the verge of tears. "I didn't think anybody could hear me."

"Nothing wrong with my hearing," Muriel said. "You woke me from a sound sleep."

"I'm stuck in here! I can barely breathe!"

"My stars," she said. "How in the world did you get in there?"

"I fell. I was up on the roof."

"You fell."

"I had my legs dangling into the chimney, and I slipped and fell inside."

"Good Lord."

"I hit the back of my head when I fell. It knocked me out. When I came to, I was stuck in the chimney."

"You went in feet first?"

"Yeah. And my arms are stuck above my head."

You can't move at all?"

"Hardly at all. My legs are trapped where the chimney narrows inside. You've got to get me out of here."

"That might be easier said than done." Muriel straightened up, a twinge in her lower back from bending over. She looked around the room, as if some solution might come into view. No help there.

She stooped over again and shouted, "How did you get up on the roof?"

"There's a ladder leaning against the house. Everything was locked up tight, so I climbed the ladder."

That damned ladder. Her handyman, Walter Bryant, had left it outdoors last time he was here, cleaning the gutters. She'd been meaning to put it away, but hadn't gotten around to it. Such chores kept piling up around the farm since George died.

"What kind of fool would climb an icy ladder on Christmas Eve?" she said. "Are you *drunk*?"

"Not anymore."

She smiled despite herself. Falling down a chimney would be a sobering experience.

"You've got to help me. I can't breathe."

"Hold on."

# UP THE CHIMNEY

STEVE BREWER

Muriel picked up the Colt and scuffed across the living floor in her slippers, headed for the foyer.

"Where are you going?" the man said. "Don't go away!"

She punched the buttons to turn off the burglar alarm. Gun at the ready, she opened the front door and peered outside. No strange vehicles were in sight. No lurking accomplices. She opened the door wide, letting the cold winter wind whistle into the house.

Muriel opened the coat closet next to the front door and pulled out her fluffy blue coat. She put the down-filled coat on over her nightgown and zipped it up to her chin. She took a flashlight down off the shelf and put it in her pocket. The Colt fit into the other pocket of the jacket, weighing it down.

She went back into the living room and shouted up the flue: "How's that? You getting some air?"

"Yes, there's a draft now, blowing past me. That helps."

She stood stooped over, listening to him gasp for breath. Cold air rushed in from the foyer, pushing the warmer air up the chimney, the only way it could leave the living room with the windows shut up tight.

## IT'S A WEIRD WINTER WONDERLAND

The furnace clicked on as the intruding cold air reached the thermostat. A waste to let the heat blow, but only temporary.

Muriel shined the flashlight up the flue, but she couldn't see any sign of the intruder. Just sooty stones and mortar blackened by decades of roaring fires. Her father had always boasted that he'd hired the best stonemason in the state to build this chimney, using stones plowed up from the surrounding fields, nearly a century ago. You don't see that kind of workmanship anymore.

"You must not be squeezed in there too tightly," she said, "if air can get past you."

"I can wiggle around a little, but I can't use my arms."

"And your feet?"

"They're dangling down past where I'm stuck. I can't bend my knees."

"Good Lord, you really are stuck then."

"If somebody could maybe go up on the roof and throw down a rope or something–"

"Up on the roof? Oh, no. That's out of the question, young man. I'm nearly eighty years old. I can't be climbing up on the roof of a two-story house."

"No, ma'am. I understand that. Is there anyone else home?"

"No, I live here alone. As if you didn't know that already."

"I didn't know, I swear," he said. "I don't know anything about you."

"You know what the inside of my chimney looks like."

That shut him up. Muriel used the pause to think about what she should do. Should she call the sheriff? Call her sons to come help? She really didn't want *anybody* climbing up on her frosty roof at midnight with one idiot stuck in the chimney. She didn't need people falling off the roof, too. That would ruin Christmas for sure.

"Call the fire department," said the man in the chimney. "They know how to get people out of places when they're stuck."

"Oh, no, we don't want to do that. We've got a volunteer fire department here in Guthrie County. Mostly those three McClarty brothers, who are too stupid to be employable. Fat slobs who have no business climbing a ladder."

"I don't know anything about that," the unseen man said, pleading in his voice. "I'm not from here."

"Trust me. I know those McClarty boys."

"I'm willing to take my chances. Just call somebody, anybody, to come help me out of here."

## IT'S A WEIRD WINTER WONDERLAND

Muriel could barely hear him over the roaring furnace. She shivered as the icy wind blew up her nightgown and stung her legs. It must be in the teens outside, and that prairie wind never ceased. Still, she shuffled over to the thermostat and turned down the dial so the furnace clicked off.

"Hello?" the man shouted. "Hello? Are you still there?"

"I'm here," Muriel said as she returned to the fireplace. "You still getting a breeze up there?"

"Yeah, but it's hard to breathe. There's soot and stuff."

"I've been meaning to get that chimney swept, but I keep putting it off. Of course, I didn't expect I'd be getting company that way."

Silence from the chimney.

"What's your name, young man?"

"Wayne."

"Wayne what?"

"Um, does my last name matter?"

"Of course it does. Do I know your people?"

"I told you, I'm not from around here. I was just passing through."

"Where are you from?"

"Kansas City."

"Where's your car?"

# UP THE CHIMNEY

"I was hitchhiking, out on the highway. I saw your porch light. It was a lot farther from the highway than it looks."

"This flat country will fool you that way," Muriel said. "So you decided to hike all the way down my gravel road – two miles – to check out that porch light. To see if there was something you could steal."

No answer. She could only hope that he was too embarrassed by his own actions to speak. Muriel liked to believe people were still capable of shame, even in this day and age.

"I'm really sorry," he said finally. "I made a big mistake. But you've got to help me."

"Uh-huh. We'll see about that."

It was freezing in here, the winter wind blowing through the open door as if it were bringing the dark night itself inside.

Muriel creaked into the kitchen, ignoring the cries of "Ma'am? Ma'am?" coming from the chimney. She set the kettle on the stove to boil, then puttered around the kitchen, getting out the teabags and a cup and a spoon. When the kettle whistled, she took it off the fire. She always liked the way the shriek mellowed to an alto as the stream of steam escaped.

# IT'S A WEIRD WINTER WONDERLAND

She poured the hot water into the cup, over the teabag waiting there. The water went instantly brown, darkening further as she bobbed the teabag up and down from its string. When she judged the tea to be the perfect strength, she lifted the teabag out with the spoon and wrapped the string around and around the spoon to neatly squeeze the last of the water out of the teabag. Just the way her mother had shown her to do, when Muriel had been judged old enough for tea with the ladies. How old had she been? Twelve? Thirteen? Still a tomboy, squirming in her itchy Sunday dress. Everyone sitting in front of the fireplace, the very same fireplace where her intruder was calling for help again. As if anyone but her could hear him, way out here.

Muriel carried her cup into the living room, taking small steps so she wouldn't slosh the hot tea. She set the cup on the end table, then pulled the heavy Colt out of her pocket and set it next to the steaming cup. She settled on the sofa within reach of her tea, and wrapped a wool blanket around her arthritic knees. She didn't know how much longer she could leave the door open. They both might freeze to death in here.

Wouldn't that be something? Imagine the scandal when the authorities found a dead man in the chimney. Oh, she could just hear those nosey parkers in town, speculating about her Christmas visitor. They'd make something ugly out of it, twist a burglar's mistake into something worthy of the supermarket tabloids. In a thinly populated area like Guthrie County, everyone knew everybody's business, or thought they did, and gossip was a blood sport. Muriel had accumulated plenty of enemies over her eight decades here, and many of them were still alive to wag their sharp old tongues.

The burglar had taken up crying for help again. His voice came in sobs.

"Wayne!" she called out in her sternest maternal voice.

Silence while he pulled himself together. Then, "Yes?"

"You need to shut up, son. Nobody can hear you but me. There's nobody else for miles."

"You can call someone," he said. "The fire department—"

"Hush, Wayne. I mean it. I'm already freezing on your behalf. Wouldn't take much to get me to close the front door."

"Please don't do that. I can barely breathe up here."

"So you said."

## IT'S A WEIRD WINTER WONDERLAND

Wayne got the message. Muriel could still hear him sniffling and gasping, but he stopped yammering at her.

She sipped her tea and considered her options.

Calling the sheriff probably was the right thing to do. Let the authorities sort it out. They'd send those idiot McClarty boys up on the roof, and they'd rescue the trapped burglar – eventually. But they probably couldn't accomplish anything in the dark. If they waited until daybreak, the resulting tumult would ruin Christmas morning for her whole family.

Both her sons dutifully dragged their reluctant wives and gangly kids to the farm first thing every Christmas morning, lured by her always-perfectly-selected gifts and her delicious cinnamon rolls and homemade cider. Muriel insisted on traditional decorations, complete with mistletoe and a real tree cut fresh the day before. She made Christmas morning as special as possible because she knew it was her only opportunity to see the whole family. As soon as the gifts were unwrapped and the breakfast devoured, everyone hurried back to town to watch their football games and play with their new toys.

If the morning became all about Wayne, she'd lose her time with the grandkids. They'd scatter while she was dealing with the sheriff and the firemen and – most likely – a few reporters who'd drive out from the city. Christmas was a slow time of year for the news business. A burglar pulling a Santa Claus stunt on Christmas Eve would make an irresistible headline.

That's what I need, Muriel thought. Let everyone in the world know I'm living out here alone. The burglars would be lining up to take a crack at her.

She glanced at the Colt lying on the table beside her. If she'd caught Wayne in her house rather than in her chimney, she wouldn't have hesitated to shoot him. It would've served him right for breaking into her home. But the gun was useless now. Even if she wanted to shoot him, there was no way to angle a bullet up the flue. It could ricochet right back in her face.

Muriel caught herself. Good God, what a line of thought. As if she could kill a man just to save Christmas for the kids—

"Ma'am?" Wayne called. "Are you there?"

Muriel sipped her tea before she answered him. "I'm right here."

"Um, what are you doing?"

"Trying to decide what happens next," she said.

"Please, just call 911."

# IT'S A WEIRD WINTER WONDERLAND

"Hush, Wayne. I'm trying to think."

She thought about that tall ladder leaning against the house, likely icy and slippery as hell. Even if she could climb up there without falling to her death, what would she do up there? Throw him a rope? Then what? Wasn't like she could hoist him out of the chimney. He was wedged in there tight. And she was nearly eighty years old.

Her sons? She couldn't picture them attempting such a rescue. Both of them had gone soft in middle age, fat and happy with their office-bound lives. If Wayne was still in the chimney when they arrived, they'd insist on canceling Christmas and calling the law.

Muriel sipped her tea.

What if she could get Wayne to be quiet? If he'd promise to stay silent while the kids were here, she could wait until after they left to call the sheriff. They'd be back in town before all heck broke loose around here.

Muriel shook her head. The burglar wouldn't stay quiet, even if he promised he would. Once he heard other people talking in here, he'd start yelling for help. Ruining everything. She considered closing the damper. The metal door up in the flue could block cold air from flowing inside. Would it block sound, too? She doubted it.

# UP THE CHIMNEY

Besides, a roaring fire was part of the holiday tradition. How would she explain a cold, empty fireplace on Christmas morning? What if her sons insisted on building a fire? Wayne certainly wouldn't stay quiet then.

Muriel thought about the position of the man inside the chimney. If there was room for cool air to pass around him, did that mean smoke would go out, too? Say he died in the chimney, from a heart attack or suffocation or something, would she still be able to use the fireplace?

She thought about the smokehouse that her father had maintained when she was a girl, a mysterious shed, always kept locked, where he'd turn whole hogs into smoked delicacies. George had torn the shed down years before, but Muriel still remembered the aroma from the smokehouse's blackened flue.

She supposed a body in a chimney would be a lot like a pig in a smokehouse. The body would shrivel in the heat and smoke, the fat rendered and the skin baked into leather. Leaving ever more room for the smoke to get out the flue.

Why, a family could have a dead burglar in their chimney for years and never know it. She wondered how many chimneys across the nation were stuffed with dried-out corpses.

## IT'S A WEIRD WINTER WONDERLAND

Muriel smiled. Santa Claus would be sure to skip those houses.

After a minute, she said, "Wayne?"

"Yes, ma'am?"

"Why aren't you with your family?"

"What?"

"It's Christmas, Wayne. Most people spend Christmas with their families, not stuck in a chimney in the middle of nowhere."

"Oh. I don't really have much family left. Both my parents are dead."

"That's too bad."

"Yeah, well, we didn't get along that well anyway," he said.

"No?"

"I've always been the black sheep of the family. Getting in trouble with the cops and getting fired from jobs and stuff like that."

"Every family has its problem child. Don't you even *call* your relatives on Christmas?"

"We don't really keep in touch."

"That's a shame."

Wayne coughed and gasped inside the chimney.

"So much soot," he said. "It's in my eyes and my nose."

"It's probably getting cold in there, too," Muriel said. "With the wind blowing up the flue."

# UP THE CHIMNEY STEVE BREWER

"My teeth are chattering."

"I'm freezing, too," she said. "I'll turn the heat back up."

She set the blanket aside and got to her feet and shuffled in her slippers to the thermostat on the wall. She turned it up until she heard the burner in the basement furnace come to life. Soon, warm air would flow from all the vents. She needed to shut the front door.

Muriel went to the foyer and looked into the front yard. Still no sign of any cars. The gravel road, her lifeline to the highway, disappeared into the darkness. She thought about Wayne walking along that lonely road, shivering in the cold, his sights set on her house, larceny in his heart.

She shut the door.

Still bundled in her puffy blue coat, she went back into the living room for her teacup, pausing at the fireplace to shout up to Wayne, "You ought to be warmer in a minute."

He said something, but she was already turning away, headed back to the kitchen. She'd need another cup of tea to stay awake the next few hours, maybe even a cup of coffee. She rarely drank coffee anymore, it was too acidic, but these were special circumstances that required extra energy. She still had cinnamon rolls to bake, and

## IT'S A WEIRD WINTER WONDERLAND

she needed to make her bed and get dressed before the kids arrived.

But first she had to deal with Wayne. The poor man had suffered enough.

Once the kettle whistled, she poured her tea and twirled the spoon into the string to squeeze the last drops out of the teabag. She carried the steaming cup back into the living room and set it on the table next to the Colt.

"How you doing, Wayne?"

"Can't breathe so good." He coughed a couple of times. "You've got to call somebody—"

"Let me ask you something, Wayne. When you were a little boy, did you believe in Santa Claus?"

"What?"

"Did you believe Santa came down the chimney and brought you toys?"

"We lived in apartment buildings when I was a kid. We didn't have chimneys. We had fire escapes."

"But you believed in Santa? You believed in being a good boy so you'd get presents at Christmas?"

Silence. Then Wayne said, "You want the truth?"

"Of course."

"I never really believed any of that stuff. I mean, we visited Santa Claus at the mall, but I always saw the man behind the beard."

"That's too bad. Christmas is so magical for most children. You really missed something."

"I guess so." He coughed some more. "Did you close the door or something? It's getting harder to breathe."

"You said you were cold. I'm warming up the place."

He coughed and sobbed.

"You've got to do something," he said. "I'm dying in here."

"All right, son. Take it easy."

Muriel stripped off the puffy coat and tossed it onto the sofa. The air was cold on her bare arms, but it would be warmer soon. She took a bracing sip of tea and turned to the fireplace, using the poker to push yesterday's ashes out of the way.

Firewood lay stacked beside the hearth. She chose a dry chunk of oak for the centerpiece and dropped it into the fireplace with a loud "thunk!"

"What was *that*?"

She ignored the question, saying instead, "I've got five grandchildren, Wayne, still young because my sons waited so long to start their families. I think the oldest two grandsons probably don't believe anymore, but the other three, they're still young enough to believe it all."

"What are you talking about, ma'am?"

"Santa Claus," she said. "My littlest grandkids still believe that Santa brings presents down the chimney at Grandma's house. They can't wait to come see me every year."

Next to the stack of split oak, Muriel kept an old coffee can full of pine shards, splinters of oily wood from the heart of the tree. George always said it made the best kindling. She chose several pieces and leaned them against the log in the fireplace, leaving room for air to pass between them.

"I guess the kids are in for a surprise this year," Wayne rasped, "unless you can get me out of here before morning. A man up the chimney sure would mess up Christmas."

"My thoughts exactly."

The weekly *Guthrie Gazette* was on the coffee table where she'd left it the day before. Mostly Christmas ads, so it hadn't taken long to read. Muriel plucked a few pages from the slender stack and crumpled them into fist-sized balls. She stooped over and wedged the paper balls among the kindling.

# UP THE CHIMNEY

STEVE BREWER

"Ma'am? What's that noise? What are you doing?"

"I've got to save Christmas for my grandchildren. At my age, this could be the last Christmas I get with them. I can't let you ruin that, Wayne."

"What are you gonna do?"

Muriel didn't answer. She struck a match on the hearthstone and touched the flame to the wadded newspaper. Smoke curled upward from the burning paper, the flue still drawing well, despite the obstacle in the chimney. The kindling quickly caught fire.

Wayne coughed and choked against the smoke. He cussed and pleaded and begged, but Muriel was done listening. She carried the Colt upstairs and put it away. Then she shucked her nightgown and put on the clothes she'd picked out the night before. Green stretch pants and a red sweater decorated with white snowflakes and reindeer. A fuzzy red Santa hat set on her head at a jaunty angle.

By the time she came back downstairs, ready to bake her famous cinnamon rolls, Wayne wasn't making a sound. The oak log was burning now, and the blaze roared in the fireplace, throwing orange light around the room.

# IT'S A WEIRD WINTER WONDERLAND

Muriel sniffed. A whiff of the smokehouse in the air, but it probably would be gone by the time the grandkids arrived. The whole house would smell like cinnamon rolls and cider by then.

She plugged in the colorful lights on the Christmas tree, filling the living room with their cheerful glow.

As she went to the kitchen, humming to herself, she paused long enough to turn down the thermostat.

The old house was toasty warm.

# Wreckless Eyeballing

## David James Keaton

Our mother was the one who ruined Christmas for everybody. Here in the hometown we never left, she came up with this idea of dialing license numbers so you could talk to any car on the highway.

Here's how it worked: As long as you could see the plate, you could punch in the combination of letters or numbers on your phone and be instantly connected to another driver. It was more like calling the car than the driver, which made you more likely to do it. It also seemed like a match made in Heaven, as most phone numbers and most plates both had seven characters. Our mother got the idea from the orientation video they showed her at her new job for the Kentucky License Bureau - a quick history of license plates and how, before there were so many cars on the road, the identification tag was just a short series of letters, almost always a word that could be easily remembered.

She worked there at least 48 hours, the longest she'd ever remained employed, and, coincidentally, the average amount of time between gun-related road-rage encounters in the United States.

"License plates are just like the first phone numbers!" our mother announced to that VCR/TV combo in the License Bureau break room, as the light bulb began flashing over her head. She tried to get through her next two days of training, but she found this impossible when her brain was storming with new ideas. She was obsessed with the new phones, small and thin as Communion wafers now. She remembered when the wafers were as thick as Christmas cookies, but everyone told her this was a false memory from growing up small and broke.

Most cars were given names, she realized, phones too, like pets or wives. Our mother decided this was probably why those older vehicles in movies were in such pristine condition, since you were more likely to take care of a machine with a name instead of a number. If it had a name, you might even be inclined to give a neighbor's car an affectionate pat on the hood on the way by, maybe tell them damn kids to stop throwing their football over it, maybe even stop to wipe off a patch of bird shit with your own hand. Seemed reasonable. But we didn't have the heart to tell her the only reason cars were so shiny in the movies was because those were toys lining streets no bigger than a sandbox. They were merely toys, as new as the ones piled up under the Christmas tree. And one day, every car ended up rusted out, in garages or abandoned car washes, no matter what name you gave it. But toys looked big from the right angle, just like the trees, just like Priest who laid that delicious Frisbee on her tongue, and our mother never understood a forced perspective. Only her own.

She told us that once she stole a whole bag of Communion wafers, and when she got busted, she piled them on a plate on Christmas Eve, next to a tall glass of milk, spilling over the brim. They were gone in the morning, she said, which didn't help her confusion. That's right around when she started trying to call Santa on the telephone, accusing whoever answered of vast conspiracy. And that was on a huge, rotary phone, too, a technology that meant commitment.

# IT'S A WEIRD WINTER WONDERLAND

But despite our bizarre urge to spin such a complicated lie as Santa Claus during our children's formative years, our mother made connections other people didn't. And she was convinced her new idea would catch on fast, just like that nutty text messaging all us kids were doing these days, and several cellular companies agreed with her. Hell, even NORAD had already developed a Santa Sleigh Tracker, which, embarrassingly enough, had already been mistaken for a Russian first-strike at least twice by our President.

Similar to texting, her concept turned out to be the absolute worst of all worlds, not only causing a driver's terrible instincts to quickly surface, but giving a convenient voice to these urges, as well. People discovered the only reason highways weren't piled even higher with more gun-toting, trigger-twitching, road-rage wreckage was because that anger for every perceived insult - cutting people off, driving too slow, driving too fast, just driving too *wrong*, etc. - was usually quenched harmlessly with a rehearsed glare or obscene gesture from the relative safety of your own rolling cell. Sure, the gestures increased exponentially depending on one driver's perception of weakness, "babies on board," or new car smells still perceptible on the highway from three car lengths away (the exact distance recommended to avoid tailgating), but - excepting the off chance that two deaf people would have a clash on the turnpike and start throwing page after page of hand signs and shadow animals out their windows - drivers normally had no real voice for their frustrations, except for a fast "Fuck you" followed by the only logical response, "Fuck you, too!".

Message sent. Message received.

Dialing the license plate in front of you and instantly getting a car on the phone changed everything. They never should have debuted it during the holidays, when traffic and people were at their worst.

Our mother's brainchild went nationwide on Christmas Eve 2018.

Okay, maybe not quite nationwide. Still, a nightmarishly ambitious tech-*bro* - inspired by "Hubris," the hugely popular app that accidently turned the average Joe into a taxi driver/rapist - jumped on board to help connect every stranger on the road in the state. She always resented joining forces with this guy, but considered him a necessary evil. They had big plans, treating our small town like a canary in a gold mine. More like a canary someone forgot on the hood of their car, come to think of it. She felt like it was taking back the road, opening lines of communication, a good-hearted disarmament pact. Or something. Because while, on the surface it seemed like the highways were a playground for us boys, women dominated every road. This wasn't wishful thinking or a political statement, our mother explained. This was simple statistics. Hard numbers. It was just hard to see them because, even with their driver's seats up straight as an arrow, they laid low. But this will change, she told us.

She didn't make a whole lot of money at this venture, but it was enough to divorce my dad, and certainly enough cash to ignore the collateral damage. We thought she'd be sensitive to actually causing road-rage incidents, especially after her injury.

The rest of the population didn't have her drive, her special sort of tunnel vision. So, after lots of hand-wringing and bullet-riddled pile-ups in the drainage ditches, after all the fist fights through the flowers and cat tails along the sides of the roads, the bodies in the gutters, the blood-n-oil Jackson Pollocks across the yellow lines, and the strips of chrome decorating every gas-reeking bush along the highway, a new law was passed fast. It said you couldn't talk on your phone anymore while driving, let alone call another car.

It was quickly passed in other States, too, under the reasonable assumption that phones had always been a dangerous distraction, like listening to headphones, doing crossword puzzles, thumb wrestling, you name it. But few people knew the real reason for the law, fewer than the fools who still believed Santa Claus could navigate that level of holiday traffic.

It was all because of our mother.

All because a phone was more like a weapon than a tool during that one terrible winter in our hometown.

Even now, if you answer your phone too fast around here, you might find yourself in a quick-draw situation with a state trooper. You're standing next to a parked vehicle and flip open your cell, fast as Captain Kirk, you could be tackled to thwart a suicide attempt. But who are we kidding? Those motherfuckers will probably shoot you anyways and call it Seasonal Defective Disorder.

To this day, people on the street are pushing for more restrictions to curb road rage. There's talk of the law against tinted windows being repealed, massive subwoofer installations

# IT'S A WEIRD WINTER WONDERLAND

rewarded, and people are encouraged to have as many suction-cup teddy bears clinging to their back windshields as possible, in order to distract drivers from locking eyes at dangerous speeds, maybe to encourage fuzzier, happier thoughts on the roads. Hell, we even heard rumors of them bringing back that show *Pimp My Ride*. A documentary on prostitution was shown at our last town hall meeting, where college students – half-jokingly at best - suggested we adopt the hustler's blanket policy of "no reckless eyeballing" for their stable, sometimes referred to as their "Elves on the Shelves," women who had to learn quickly the golden rule about keeping their gaze focused solely on the curb.

While we learned a lot that day during the Q&A, like how a citizen's arrest might never be quite as serious as young women being put under "pimp arrest," both punishments turned out to be surprisingly similar when pranksters listed them side-by-side next to those double doors of our courthouse, right under the Ten Commandments:

*"Look down at your feet, your hands, or the road at all times. And do not make eye contact with the mark unless there is a car coming toward you. Do not make eye contact with a pimp, under any circumstances."*

# WRECKLESS EYEBALLING         DAVID JAMES KEATON

Our mother bragged that she had precisely the same rules stamped on a business card, long before local governments adopted them, and we decided to believe her. Rules to live by, we agreed.

They still call the DMV the "DMZ" around here, and in driver's ed. class, you now hear recent statistics suggesting how you're just as likely to have your eyes enucleated by the car keys clenched in someone's fist during a road-rage experience as you are to be struck by lightning. Which, as it turns out, happens constantly when you're in a car. Only we cannot feel this. One of the benefits of being electrically grounded by rubber tires - which, it turns out - was almost as important to our successful upbringing as being grounded by our mother. The silver lining they don't mention when you receive your license, is that a human eye hanging from its optic nerve (as long as it retains some of the ciliary muscle around the cornea, of course) makes a handy and expressive souvenir. It can hang from your key chain at least as long as your car alarm fob. Maybe not as personalized as those tiny state license plates you can pick up in gas stations - the ones they never seem to have with *your* first name (and our mother knows this because she looked through every damn one of them) - but some religions maintain that memories are stored in the iris, rather than the brain. Of course, some believe that a Christmas cookie is a fucking corpse, so who are we to play favorites. Believe in what you want.

As horrific as this kind of injury seems, in our town it brought us closer together. This sort of injury was somehow better.

They say the human head can send signals to the body for up to five minutes after it's detached. It turned out an eyeball reports back to your brain for years. Getting one plucked out during an assault also serves as a handshake afterwards. More than a handshake, actually. More of a hazy impression in your good eye that you're now living someone else's life. Or at least their car's. For anyone carrying those key chains, it's a sort of a deterrent. Like the fake testicles the female squid flash so the males leave them the fuck alone. Like those eyes on the backs of caterpillars that trick birds into thinking they're snakes. Like the reindeer's nose that glows as red as a taillight if a bumper punches the little bastard just right. Too hard, and the noses blink out forever. Too soft, and it doesn't learn anything.

Our mother recently tried to pitch her original idea to another phone company, in the next state over this time, where they shoot holes in streetlights just to make them change. And even though the glut of vanity plates across the country might pose a problem, she was pretty sure they were gonna go for it, despite the fact that it might be doomed by complication one day, without enough numbers. Communication was traditionally revered, she admitted, but calling the wrong number could be fatal for both drivers, no matter how much road was between them.

She couldn't, in good conscious, play matchmaker to humanity forever.

But she'd continue to sell her key chains. They were great stocking stuffers, she would explain, and they'd always made her enough money to get by, certainly more money than the jewelry she used to create, and there was always plenty to harvest on the sides of the roads during the holidays when everyone was looking at everyone all wrong, especially when she saw herself reflected in their anger, or reflected in the change in their pockets. Selling them was always going to be a little trickier than plucking them though, not just because Christmas was forever fucked up after what she'd done, but she swore people trusted her more than most.

We certainly did, and not just because of her eye patch. Believed in her, you could say.

## IT'S A WEIRD WINTER WONDERLAND

# Saint Nikki's Revenge
## Laurie Zottmann

My mother told me I'd regret my career. If she had her way, we'd all be servants of the church. But I think one Pastor Karen in the world is enough.

She was right, though. I am sitting here in a cheaply carpeted circle, regretting the choices that brought me here.

"Well, *I* think you're being dramatic," one of the nastier group members says to another. "It can't be THAT hard. Just eat more vegetables."

The dramatic one blows her nose, so swollen from crying that nothing comes out. "I *dold* you," she says, "they don't put much produce in the food hampers. It's all peanut butter and Kraft dinner."

Nasty rolls her eyes.

I swallow a scream.

# IT'S A WEIRD WINTER WONDERLAND

This is what affordable mental health support looks like. The Community Counselling Society, where I am an unpaid intern, claims to provide our clients with the tools to live better. But really, we're just running repeat episodes of a fucking gong show.

The sweet one looks at me. When she sees I'm not going to intervene, she jumps in with a helpful, "How about exercise? A good swim always clears my head."

Drama buries her sobs in a sticky fistful of Kleenex.

"Oh, yeah!" Nasty says. "Tell us more about how you use 'a good swim' to clear your head. What are you swimming in? Soft serve?"

Sweet's mouth drops open, compressing her chins. I close my eyes and rub my temples.

"You guys need to masturbate," I mutter.

That's the moment the room goes quiet. I open my eyes. The ladies are staring at me.

"Are you serious?" asks Drama.

My heart bashes in my ears. *Am I really going here?*

"How amazing would it be if you could escape to pleasure, whenever you need it?"

The women's faces twitch.

"Aren't you sick of talking about exercise and healthy eating? Shit you can't afford, can't control, and can't make yourself give a fuck about? Let's talk about getting our rocks off."

Drama covers her wide-mouthed laughter with an embarrassed hand.

"Seriously, you guys," Sweet says. "How can we pull this off at the shelter? Privacy isn't exactly a thing."

"In the shower?" Nasty, of all people, suggests.

I am paralyzed with delight as the women start brainstorming. They talk about the shower schedule at the women's shelter, the best times to use the communal bathroom, and which Starbucks has the quietest single-person restroom.

By the time the session ends, my heart is bursting. The women file out in a huddle, whispering conspiratorially. Nasty nods at me on her way by. Drama is the last one out.

"Merry Christmas, Nikki. And thank you." Her eyes sparkle.

I want to hug her so bad. When she's gone, I wipe a few tears. Until today, I've hated this internship and questioned my resolve to become a registered psychologist.

My mother's voice rings back to me from the day I quit bible college for *that Freudian claptrap*.

## IT'S A WEIRD WINTER WONDERLAND

"Nobody is Freudian anymore, Mom."

"They're still a bunch of perverts. You'll get what you deserve," she'd said.

Maybe I will.

🎄

Every Saturday morning, I wake with my guts cramped with dread. But I force myself to show up for my mother's sermons at the Seventh-Day Adventist church. Apostasy and hellfire. Jesus, the slaughtered lamb. Pastor Karen, the great and terrible.

GreatWhiteGirth once asked me why I keep going back. I couldn't answer. I just can't stop.

🎄

The clinic is dark at 4:30pm.

As I walk past the intern supervisor's office, the door springs open.

"Nikki," Roberta says. "We need to talk."

My stomach sinks.

Roberta steps back and holds the door for me. A whiff of stale sweat drifts up to me from her raised arm. Roberta lowers herself into her chair. I watch the wattle jiggle under her chin and wait for the bad news.

"I don't understand why you can't follow protocol," she says.

My face flushes hot pink.

"Could you be more specific?" I ask, determined to stand behind the only counselling advice I've given so far that lit a spark in those women.

Roberta lowers her eyes back to mine. "That's not an appropriate topic for group counselling."

"What topic, Roberta? Masturbation? Bailing the boat? Diddling the skittle? Why shouldn't we talk about it? Does it make you too horny? Are you so swampy in your slacks right now that the minute I leave, you're gonna shove your whole fist up the ol' soup hole?"

I have been fired.

On Christmas Eve.

Good thing this gig wasn't paying my rent. I walk out of the clinic in a trance and don't notice the arctic gale sweeping me through the rush-hour streets to get home.

When I unlock my apartment door, I am greeted with an impatient red strobe: the voicemail light on my land line. It glitters off 450 square feet of twinkling lights and garland that I call home. My shitbox flat is festively adorned 365 days a year. My little piece of crazy. Pastor Karen always said the holidays were nothing but a road to damnation, paved in tinsel. I disagree.

Since my escape from the fundamentalist thought-box, I live for snow globes, sugar cookies, and jolly old men.

A message on my landline can only mean one thing; my parents. They're the only people who refuse to call me on my mobile. I don't have the strength to face their drama. Not yet.

I drag a kitchen chair in front of the fridge and pull a dusty bottle of Patrón from the cupboard above. The very first bottle of fire water I ever bought. It's been there since last Christmas.

Pouring a couple of fingers into the bottom of a cleanish drinking glass, I think about the look on Roberta's face today. The way her neck wattle trembled as she wrote me off. I pour some more.

That damned voicemail still flashes. I grab the bottle, leaving the glass on the counter as I wobble to the couch.

My eyes water as I hold the booze in my mouth. It burns my inner cheeks in a weirdly pleasant way. I stopped caring ages ago about what Jesus would think about my life. But I still think about my mother.

# SAINT NIKKI'S REVENGE — LAURIE ZOTTMANN

The tequila fires down my throat and into my stomach. My empty stomach. I forgot my lunch this morning.

I check the clock and see I've got fifteen minutes before my first call. I stand up, thinking to grab the forgotten turkey sandwich from the fridge, then remember the message light.

I groan and stomp over to the phone.

"Nikki?" croaks my father. "Baby. It's me. Your father. Your dear old *DAAAAAAAAD*."

He's drunk. In the history of answering machines, I believe my father has yet to leave a sober message.

"Hate to tell you this, Sweetheart, but I have *terrrrrrrible* news."

My father *loves* to give me terrible news.

"It's your mother, Nikki. She's a whore."

Not this again.

"She ruined our family!"

Then he falls silent. Just when I start to wonder if Dad fell asleep, his voice comes back in a lurch. "I love you, Sweetheart." He snorts and grunts, and starts to cry. "Daddy loves you. Don't forget. Ok? You're a good girl, Nikki. You're better than her. I raised you right. *Wishhhh* I married you. Good, good girl."

He punctuates it with a loud belch.

# IT'S A WEIRD WINTER WONDERLAND

"See you tomorrow, Kiddo. Bring scotch." And then he hangs up.

I close my eyes and squeeze my forehead. Dad accuses mom of cheating about three times a year. And I wish it were true.

I pound the seven key. Hard.

"Message deleted," the mailbot responds. "Next message:"

"Hello, Nicole? It's Pastor Karen. I mean – your mother. I understand your father has left you a... confusing message. I just want to confirm, lunch is *on* for tomorrow. Right after the service. I'll see you at the sanctuary at 9:45. Don't be late, Nicole. And for Jesus' love, don't dress like a whore."

"Sent today at..." says the mailbot.

I mash down that seven-to-delete like it was my mom's collapsing trachea.

"*Fuck the both of you!*" I scream and hurl the handset into the wall. It dents the plaster.

"*Shit!*"

That's gonna cost me when I move out. If I ever have enough money to leave.

*Doop-dee-doop*

The Skype app on my phone announces a call.

"*Fuck*," I shout as I dash into my bedroom. I rip off my shirt, yank the wig off the hanger and lunge toward the coffee table.

# SAINT NIKKI'S REVENGE

LAURIE ZOTTMANN

*Doop-dee-doop blop-blop*

"I'm here!" I say as I fling my laptop open and pound the spacebar to wake it up.

*Doo-doop-de-doop*

"Don't hang up!" I plead.

Finally, the screen flickers on.

"I'm here, Longhandle. Whew. Holy fuck. Alright. St. Nikki is here. Let's have a White Christmas, shall we?"

Longhandle69 doesn't respond. His video feed is blank. That's part of the arrangement. He can see me, but I can't see him. It works better that way for both of us.

But his silence is unusual.

"Um, are you there?" I ask. "Longhandle?"

"It's Mr. Long," he finally replies. "We decided that last time. The contract has been amended, has it not?"

I slap my forehead. "Sorry! You're absolutely right—Mr. Long. Of course." I take a deep breath, get my bearings, and sweeten my voice. "Have you been a good boy, Mr. Long?"

"Ottoman," he barks. "*Ooo-ttoman!!*"

His safe word.

"Is something the matter?" I ask.

"Your hair is crooked, you came on late, and I *hate* being called a good boy. That's a hard no. It makes me feel like a dog. You ought to know better."

I press the heel of my palm into my forehead and sigh.

"Ah... Mr. Long. You're right. Absolutely right. I have to apologize, it's been an extremely long day..."

Mr. Long cuts me off.

"If I wanted to hear about your day, I would *date* you, Nikki."

I sigh again. I know what's coming.

"I'd like to discontinue our arrangement," Mr. Long says. "This isn't working."

"Alright. Just drop me an email to confirm it in writing, and I'll cancel your next payment.

There is a heartbeat of silence.

"I will, you know," he mumbles. "It's over. This time, for real."

I'm pretty sure it's not. These threats are Mr. Long's favourite part of our routine. It takes the sting out of my fuckup, knowing how much he loves to watch me wallow in remorse.

"I understand, Mr. Long." I exaggerate my trembling lower lip for the camera. "It's been a pleasure working with you."

Mr. Long starts to breathe audibly. "Good night, Nikki."

# SAINT NIKKI'S REVENGE  LAURIE ZOTTMANN

"Merry Christmas," I whisper, my voice cracking theatrically.

Longhandle69 ends the call. I shake my head. I know what he's doing right now, and it isn't typing up a notice of cancellation.

I stare at myself on the video feed. Longhandle was right—my platinum wig is totally cock-eyed, exposing my bottle-coloured ebony-mocha locks above my left ear.

The mess doesn't end with my hair. This morning's mascara has sloughed off my lashes and settled under my eyes in ghoulish smudges. A zombie webcam girl. In a depressingly utilitarian bra. Fuck. I didn't have time to grab my show bra. This is totally off-brand.

I lower my forehead onto the coffee table and groan, feeling my pores open in the trapped steam of my breath.

I remind myself that I have another call in ten minutes. I'm going to put my game face on and do the one goddamned thing that actually makes me feel like sane human being.

My glass of tequila looks neglected. I suck down the remaining six ounces or so in two desperate swallows. The velvety fire hisses against the back of my throat.

# IT'S A WEIRD WINTER WONDERLAND

My next client is GreatWhiteGirth. He's my only watcher who likes to turn his camera on.

Blood flares in my cheeks, as an image flashes in my mind from our last session. I'd nearly caved to the urge to offer Girth another round. For free. In person.

I wash my face and apply a fresh coat of mascara as I picture Girth: the sparkling white-greys sprinkled copiously through this long, brown waves; the long moustache and beard; and those wide brown eyes that flash between sympathy and mischief in a way that makes my stomach drop.

A wave of dizziness washes over me. I wonder if six ounces is a lot of tequila to chug on an empty stomach.

I hastily swipe the unmade eye with a few globs of mascara. Then I tug on my red-sequined, fur-trimmed bra.

*Doop-dee-doop* my phone and my laptop sing.

I click, "Answer with Video."

The screen flickers and resolves onto a scene I know well. In front of a teal-painted wall, there is a black leather couch. And sitting on the black leather couch is an olive-skinned man. He's naked except for a red velvet Santa hat. And a grin.

"Merry Christmas!" GreatWhiteGirth chuckles. "But it's always Christmas at Saint Nikki's house, isn't it?"

I smile, and my vision blurs.

"Have you been a good boy, GreatWhiteGirth?" I ask in a voice that I hope sounds self-possessed.

"Oh, yes. *Very* good, Saint Nikki," Girth answers.

I raise my eyebrow. "Oh, really? Because my data logs show that you've been doing some naughty things, Mr. Girth. Very naughty, indeed."

Girth's face drops solemnly. "You know about it, then?"

"I see you when you're sleeping, remember? I know when you're awake. And I know when you've been feverishly polishing the North Pole, Mr. Girth."

"You do?" Girth says, smiling as he leans back, making the leather squeak.

"It's just not proper," I moan, trailing my fingertips between my breasts and down my belly. "You're supposed to wait for me. That's the rule."

Girth slides the tip of his middle finger up his shaft.

The room wobbles. I grab the edge of the coffee table to pull myself up. With only my festive panties in view of the camera, I slide my thumbs into the strap on each hip, and slip them unhurriedly down my thighs.

Girth groans.

"Tsk, tsk, Mr. Girth. Now, I can't hardly come sit on your knee and let you tickle my beard if you keep breaking the rules," I sigh. "It wouldn't be fair to the other boys and girls."

I hear a rhythmic beat of slapping skin. When I kneel down to take a peek at the video, Girth is looking straight at me. My cheeks flush.

"Hey!" he says. "Now who's being naughty? You'd better get those fingers wet, Missy. I'm not paying you to watch."

I tilt my head.

"Aren't you?" I smirk. Then I open my mouth, lay my middle finger on my tongue, and close my lips around it as I slowly pull it out.

"*Uuuugh*," Girth grunts, closing his eyes. Then he sighs. "You make my bad days evaporate, you know that?"

I stare at him, resting back with his eyes closed. Carefree. Jealousy wrinkles my forehead. I envy the expensive couch, in what appears to be an expensive home. I envy his power to pay for sex entertainment, rather than having to put on the show. I resent his freedom and security. But most of all, I covet that expression on his face. He is not struggling with doubt, or voices of shame. He isn't filled with rage about painful memories that should have been filled with love.

He's just... *being*.

"Oh, I want to do such things to you," Girth goes on, his eyes still shut.

It's too much. Before I can stop myself, I burst into angry tears and bury my face in my hands. The skin-slapping stops. I hear a couch-leather squeak.

"Oh, hey," he says gently. "Hey, Nikki? What happened? Are you okay?"

I look up and see him leaning into the camera with a look of grave concern. Its seriousness is slightly diluted by the fuzzy red hat on his head and the shiny pink helmet in his hand.

I smile at him woozily.

"Fuck me, Jesus," I croak. GreatWhiteGirth's eyebrow pops up.

"Uhhh! I didn't... I mean... not *the* Jesus." I grab my skull in both hands to stop my brain from sloshing.

Girth chuckles. "It's cool. I can be your dark saviour." His mouth is smiling, but his pupils swell in a way that raises the hair on my neck.

I am about to object frantically, but I pause. I let myself imagine doing more than simply taking His name in vain. I could take Him. Do I want to play-fuck the son of God who died for my sins?

I imagine laying my head on Girth's chest, hearing his heart beat while he wraps his arms around me, pressing his throbbing cock against my belly and washing away all my sins with his flesh and fluids. The body of Christ. My nipples ache.

I look into Girth's eyes, feeling mesmerized. His smile quiets the panicked canary in my chest. I feel like I could tell him anything.

"My mother would sell her soul to fuck Jesus," I whisper. Girth's eyes widen.

I rub my temples. My thoughts circle in wobbly loops and I try to follow the idea through the swirl.

"What if you Jesus-fucked Pastor Karen?" I mused aloud. "Maybe it would thaw her frozen heart."

Girth laughs. "Like a Disney movie? From what you've told me about her, I don't think a single, epic shag could turn her pinched pussy upside-down," he says.

I close my eyes and try to picture it.

But I can't visualise my mother in Girth's arms. Instead, I see a memory.

It's the middle of the night. She thinks everyone's asleep, and hasn't bothered to fully

# SAINT NIKKI'S REVENGE       LAURIE ZOTTMANN

close the door to her study. A slice of blue light from her monitor stabs into the hallway. I press my face up to the crack.

A video is playing silently on Pastor Karen's computer: the whipping scene from The Passion of the Christ. I watch my mother lean back, slide down in her chair, and slip her hand inside the waistband of her polyester slacks. Onscreen, Jim Caviezel's mouth opens as the lash tears his back to bloody ribbons. The only sound that reaches me is the steady music of Pastor Karen's creaky chair and her heavy breath.

"Holy shit, Girth!" I say. "That's who you remind me of."

"Jesus?" he says.

"Jim Caviezel," I answer. "You are my mother's fantasy come to life."

Girth laughs.

I don't.

"You seriously want me to fuck your mother?" he asks, and watches me carefully.

The dark thing inside me raises its eyebrow. The more I drunkenly squint at it, the more the idea of having Girth hate-fuck my mother feels right. A little spot of heat flares between my breasts, where my crucifix used to lay. I touch the spot and picture a thumb drive hanging there, loaded with a video of the mighty Pastor Karen getting thoroughly profaned.

"Would you do it?" I ask him. He frowns and scrubs both palms over his head. "Yes. But you would owe me," he adds, *"big time."*

My ears thunder with a rush of blood and the next thing I know, I'm bracing myself against the stiff breath of winter outside Pastor Karen's well-kept secret: a depressing bar in a bad part of town. This is where she goes when Dad thinks she's cheating. I guess this time, she will be.

A dark grey BMW glides into the parking lot and GreatWhiteGirth steps out. He's shorter than I expected.

He walks over to me and looks me up and down. "I wouldn't have pegged you for a blonde."

"I'm not," I reply. "This is my Pastor Karen wig. Just look for this, but dressed neck-to-toe in the Jessica line from Sears.

Girth shudders, and then pulls open the grimy front door of the pub. "After you."

He puts his hand on the small of my back, and I can feel the heat of his palm, like he's been juggling hot coals. I stumble. Girth takes my arm.

"We're getting you some water," he says, and guides me to an empty table.

*I need food,* I think, but I don't say anything.

# SAINT NIKKI'S REVENGE     LAURIE ZOTTMANN

We sit down, and Girth dazzles the waitress with a schmoozy half-smile while he orders our drinks. I stare at him, mesmerized. He seems weird in clothes. But that smile, those bottomless brown eyes, that trust-in-me beard... he'd moisten my panties if he was dressed in a HAZMAT suit.

He narrows his eyes at me.

"Quit staring. You're making me feel weird," he says.

"Sorry," I mumble.

I squint at him as the waitress returns. When she sashays away, I lean toward him.

"Why are you doing this?" I want to ask. But I don't get the chance, because right then, he reaches under the table and lays one of his fresh-from-the-oven hands on my thigh.

My stomach quivers. I reach down to touch that radiant hunk of flesh and feel something plastic. A baggie.

I bring it into the light to examine it. Girth quickly shoves my hand back below the table.

"Not here," he hisses, looking furtively left and right.

"Come on," he mutters, standing up. I slide off the tall stool and stumble after him.

My heart freefalls to my navel. "Sorry," I say. "I... I don't... usually..." I stutter along beside him, keeping my head raised high like an *extra* not-drunk person would do.

Girth steers me around the corner into a hallway and leans me up against the wall. He holds the baggie up in front of my eyes. It contains a half-dozen colourful little pills. I stare at them.

"They look like pretty candy," I say.

"It's MDMA," he says. "You said your mom was a flirter, not a cheater. It's unlikely she'll just push aside the crotch of her granny panties to admit my glistening cock."

I screw up my face.

"You're going to give Pastor Karen *ecstasy*?" This gives me the giggles.

GreatWhiteGirth looks at me seriously. "Am I?"

My scalp suddenly feels clammy. I look up into Girth's grey eyes. He's frowning, too. But not with judgement. Just gravity.

"I... I..." I slam my mouth closed and bang my fist into my lips as a wave of bile splashes up into my throat.

Tears spray out of my eyes. Everything is dark, and I feel my body whirl.

Then my stomach lurches again and I open my eyes to see a thick jet of yellow and white froth. It flies through a black horseshoe and splashes into the bottom of a big white bowl.

# SAINT NIKKI'S REVENGE     LAURIE ZOTTMANN

Warm hands brush weird, plasticky hair off my sticky brow.

Behind me, Girth's expression hasn't changed: concern without criticism. I pull some toilet paper off the roll and fold it into a square to wipe my mouth. Girth passes the baggie over my shoulder. I pick it up and squeeze the little rounds through the plastic.

I've never seen E before, but I've had it. Or something like it. I was fourteen years old. It wasn't hard to sneak out of the house that night. Karen was out, probably here, at this pub. Dad was passed out before suppertime. My first bonfire rave. Someone gave me some punch. All I remember is being thirsty. The next morning, I woke up with grass in my hair, bruises all over, and blood in my panties.

Pastor Karen found me crying in the bathroom. Her mouth was pressed so tight her lips seemed to disappear into a pucker of yellow wax cloth.

"I hope you've learned your lesson," was all she said, then she turned away and closed the door.

I turn to Girth and pass the bag back to him.

"Do it," I whisper to the pills.

Girth nods, then peels open the tiny baggie and tips a few candy-coloured pebbles into his hand.

## IT'S A WEIRD WINTER WONDERLAND

He picks one up between thick fingers and pops it into his mouth. Then he holds his palm out to me.

The snow globe in my head takes a great swish as I choose a yellow one with a happy face and lay it on my tongue.

My taste buds cringe beneath the tiny circle. Bitterness sucks up all the fluid from my tissues. I shudder and swallow.

Girth tips most of the tablets back into the bag, and tucks it into his pocket. He looks at me with a blank expression and straightens my wig. He turns to go.

"Wait!" I blurt, grabbing his sleeve. *Are we really doing this?* I want to ask. But when Girth turns to me, I catch something on his face—an impatient flare of his nostrils, maybe. The question freezes in my mouth.

"Uhhh... what if she doesn't remember afterward?"

Girth frowns and chews his lip. Then his eyes light with a smile.

"We'll send her the video," he says. "Webcams, baby. They see me when I'm sleeping..."

I close my eyes, nodding. I picture Girth's apartment from a hidden angle, looking down on that black leather couch. I can imagine my mother sitting there, but my mind can't make her reach for Girth.

"Put the file in my Dropbox. I'll send it to her tomorrow. Right before church," I say.

"Oh, I'll put a file in your dropbox, alright," Girth chuckles.

Then he leaves. The bathroom door swings behind him in diminishing arcs.

I put my hands on either side of the stall doorway and stand up. I follow Girth's invisible wake and push the door open a crack. Here I am, peeping at my mom again.

GreatWhiteGirth is sitting at the bar. Two stools to his right sits my mother. Girth leans toward Karen and gestures to the seat beside her. She nods at him. He slides over next to her and holds out his hand. She takes it and lights up her trademark 1000-watt smile. She holds onto his hand an extra beat, leans into him and mutters something toward his ear.

Girth's hearty laugh reaches me. I grit my teeth.

Girth raises his hand to the bartender and orders a drink, then gestures toward Karen. She raises her glass and nods.

The barman refills it from the soda gun: nothing but Sprite. I know this because I've followed her here before.

# IT'S A WEIRD WINTER WONDERLAND

My mother always claimed that she power-walks nightly with the church ladies. But she hasn't owned a single pair of sneakers in my lifetime. When I was sixteen, I called bullshit and tailed her for a week. She led me to this shithole bar. She did nothing but drink sodas and flirt with a bunch of greasy, low-rent alcoholics. Maybe she felt like Jesus, bumping elbows with the poor and lowly. She always left alone, though, and headed back home to rub out her sinful thoughts to images of Our Lord's bare, bloody torso.

The bartender stabs a straw into Karen's drink, drops a cherry on top, and slides it to her with a wink. Girth tilts his head toward a booth and offers Karen his arm. She beams and slips her hand through his elbow. She slides in beside him on the bench. I gag.

I watch them chat back and forth over their drinks. Girth swirls his glass on the table, but Karen cradles hers, stirring with her straw. I start to chew my fingernails. This could be a problem.

As they talk, Karen rotates her body toward Girth in subtle shifts. Her laughs get louder, and she lays her palm on his bicep. Girth whispers something in her right ear while brushing a lock of hair behind her left.

# SAINT NIKKI'S REVENGE    LAURIE ZOTTMANN

Karen leans back and her eyes close. Numb, I watch Girth's hand pass over top of her glass. Then all the sound in the room is swallowed by a rush of blood in my ears.

It's done. I've drugged my mother.

My stomach convulses. I turn and lunge back toward the toilet. My retching echoes off the porcelain floor and walls, and around the glazed curves inside my skull.

I wipe my mouth with the back of my arm.

I shuffle over to the sink and lean hard on it while I peer at my reflection. With my wheat-colored wig and pale peach button-down blouse, it's Karen staring back at me.

*I hope you learned your lesson.*

My hands throttle the edges of the sink.

The bathroom door swings open.

I take a big breath and whirl around, ready to attack... but it's Girth.

"We've got a problem," he says.

He steers me toward the door, and pushes it open a sliver. I peek out. Karen is alone in the booth, slumped over.

"What the fuck?" I wheeze.

"Not sure," Girth whispers from behind me. His breath is hot on my neck and it raises goosebumps.

"Might've dropped in a couple of tabs by mistake. Or maybe she's just taking it weird."

"Or maybe she's being punished," I mutter.

"Whatever," Girth shrugs. "How do you want to play this?"

I look around, breathing shallow. The bartender is busy at the far end of the service counter, drying glasses and talking with another patron. They are both turned to the TV, their backs to Karen. I spin around and grab Girth's collar.

"The bartender is going to know she doesn't drink!" I say.

Girth's eyes widen. "Fuck, let's move."

He pushes me out of the way and slips out the door. I dash out behind him.

As we hurry between tables, my ears start to ring. The bar seems to get farther away, and the ground rolls beneath me.

Suddenly, all the noise in the room swells. I can hear everything: lapping waves of conversation, ice cubes clinking against glass, a thousand sticky swallows. I start to pant.

Girth reaches around Karen's waist and drapes her arm over his shoulder. I totter around to her other side and grab her free arm.

# SAINT NIKKI'S REVENGE  LAURIE ZOTTMANN

Her head lolls as we walk her to the door. Just as we reach it, it opens. A crusty-looking man tries to walk in, but freezes when he sees us. His eyes dart from Karen's face to mine.

I can't breathe.

The man's face cracks into a lewd grin.

"Ha! Twins!" he chortles. "Lucky man," he adds with a wink to Girth. Then he steps back to hold the door for us.

My jaw flaps uselessly. Girth says something in a low voice, and the man guffaws again.

Next thing I know, we're inside the grey BMW. I am gripping the dash and door handle in silent terror. It feels like we are careening through the streets on a rocket-powered nightmare.

Girth turns his head slowly to me and frowns. "Are you *okaaaaaay*?" I nod laboriously. Then everything goes black.

I come-to slumped in a hard-padded accent chair. I clack my tongue. It feels like a clump of sand. I push myself to sit upright. Something slips off my lap and thuds to the floor. I look down as a plastic water bottle rolls against my foot. I pick it up and take a swig.

I hear a low moan. I look up, and see a view I know well: in front of a teal-painted wall is a black leather couch. Flopped halfway off the couch is my mother.

GreatWhiteGirth is kneeling in front of her. He puts his hands on her knees, leans in, and kisses loudly below her ear. Karen giggles and squirms feebly.

Girth straightens up and pulls his shirt over his head. The skin on his back is unbearably smooth. Never took a whip for nobody. The olive tone is warmer than it looks on-screen. Like a caramel apple. I want to lick it.

I kneel beside Girth and grab my mother by the chin, forcing her to look at me.

"Who do you think I am?" I demand. Karen blinks at me. Once. Twice. She swallows.

"You're me," she says, frowning.

"And who do you think this is?" I ask, pointing her head to Girth.

Karen regards him solemnly.

"Our Lord Saviour, Jesus Christ," she whispers, her hands swaying side-to-side before the bare torso of her soon-to-be rapist.

I let go of her face and scrub my temples. This feels wrong. I can't watch her get hate-fucked and LIKE it.

I realize I am swaying along with Karen's hands, and I bump against Girth's arm. The heat from his skin soaks through the fabric of my sleeve. I turn to him. His mouth is open. His lower lip as soft and delectable as a dinner bun.

A fireball flares in my belly, filling my panties with steam.

I turn back to Karen.

"Mom, it's me. Nikki,"

"Nikki?" she asks, shaking her head in confusion.

"Yes," I say, unbuttoning my blouse. "And you don't get to fuck Jesus Christ. He doesn't want to stick his holy cock inside you because your hateful vag would make his balls shrivel up and turn black."

"Like raisins," Girth adds over my shoulder.

My mother whimpers as I take off my wig and twirl it around my finger, then toss it onto her face. She doesn't move. I reach over and tug it off.

"I want you to watch," I say.

Girth's eyes flash and he breathes through his mouth. My crimson-mirrored bra casts devilish reflections on Pastor Karen's clammy forehead.

I take Garth's face in my hands and devour his delicious dinner-bun mouth.

He moans, slides an arm below my bottom, and lifts me up onto Karen's lap. He grinds against me then pulls back to tug my thong out from under me.

I lean back and lift my hips for him.

"*Glurk,*" Karen coughs into my ear as my shoulder shoves hard into her chest.

Girth spreads my legs astraddle my mother's, positions himself between our knees and plunges into me. He clutches my hips and rocks me on Karen's lap like a human shake weight.

The world turns pink and green and yellow. Something raps on my shoulder, a woody clap with every thrust. I look up and realize it's my mother's chin and teeth. Her head is flopping like a ragdoll. Something warm and wet drips onto my cheek, and I wipe it off, not caring whether it's drool or tears.

"*Aaagh! Aaagh! Aagh!*" I holler, each moan capped with a grunt. I look up and see Karen open-mouthed, captivated. The ear-piercing wails continue to issue from my throat.

I turn my face back to Girth. His nose wrinkles and his eyelids slide shut like a shark's just before the kill. His movements deepen. I think of a freight train picking up steam. I reach out for something to anchor me as my body thrashes back and forth. My left hand claws into the couch cushion below me, and my right clutches Karen's jaw like a vise.

Lightning zaps the soles of my feet, and the roar of sensation sweeps my consciousness away down a long, silent hallway of oblivion.

I don't emerge until the next morning.

Digital music scratches my brain. I peel one sticky eye open and see my cell phone. It's playing my morning alarm. I reach over stiffly and swipe to dismiss it.

I'm on my couch. In my apartment. My throat screams for water, but I'm not sure I could keep it down.

Girth must have driven me home. I wonder what he did with my mother. Bile splashes in my throat.

Oh god. The video.

I open my laptop and sign into Dropbox.

*Maybe I can just delete it...*

No new files.

My Skype icon has a little orange "1" on it. I click it open. It's a message from Girth.

"Last night was... surreal," it says. "Sorry about the fuckup with the recording getting switched to a live feed."

*Live feed?* I wonder. *Does that mean no one saw?*

*Doop-dee-doop*

## IT'S A WEIRD WINTER WONDERLAND

*Doop-dee-doop-blop-blop*
*Doop-doop-dee-doop*

# That's A Wrap
## Will Viharo

The beautiful naked young red-haired naked girl with the broken kneecaps crawled across the floor, leaving a trail of blood and suds (since she had been in the shower) as she pleaded for her life, finally reaching up for the telephone on the side table next to the plush sofa. The very large well-dressed man with the baseball bat responded by breaking her left arm, making her scream in agony and collapse into semi-consciousness. Earth Kitt could be heard singing "Santa Baby" on Pandora, as if everything was just peachy.

"Merry Fucking Christmas, bitch," said the equally beautiful - but far less traumatized - brunette woman standing in the hallway, watching. "Your gift is your life, as long as you stay the fuck away from that audition tomorrow, even on crutches. Happy Fucking New Year, you fucking cunt."

The large well-dressed man, and the beautiful brunette woman with intact kneecaps, walked out of the penthouse apartment, which loomed high above Sunset Boulevard. The naked red-haired naked girl with the broken kneecaps and busted left arm lived there with three other roommates, all of whom were out of town for the holidays. According to reliable rumor, she had been dating (fucking) the director of a new film and everyone assumed she would get the lead role, including the director. A few miles away in the Hollywood Hills, that same director was also lying semi-conscious on the floor with broken kneecaps, next to a blood-soaked script that was about to be re-written by new investors.

The next morning the beautiful brunette woman with intact kneecaps showed up for her audition, and nailed it – after the new director nailed her, of course. The original director had been hastily replaced due to the severity of his sudden, undisclosed "medical condition."

The beautiful brunette was thirty-five years old -which, for a female, was ancient in this business. That's why her driver's license claimed she was ten years younger. Due to her smoldering sensuous looks, enhanced by makeup and surgery, she could get away with it. Her driver's license also displayed her stage name, Miranda Mercedes, even though her birth name was Tina Romano.

Her father was Tony "The Tiger" Romano, a lieutenant for a prominent New York business organization, a group once commonly referred to as The Mafia. Now it was considered just another branch of local government, since most of the members had successfully assimilated into the business community, thanks to political camouflage bought by strategic campaign donations. And promises not to whack out certain family members

Of course, while nobody in the greater Los Angeles area was entirely aware of her connections, anyone that was unfortunate enough as to engage her in fair competition for her desired parts – whether a role in a script or a male member - was rudely introduced to one of her father's West Coast employees. The unwary victims would then belatedly suspect that they had accidentally stepped on the wrong toes, most likely planted somewhere near the Eastern seaboard. The fact that her own private "body guards" often accompanied Miranda to auditions had, nonetheless, become a whispered warning to casting directors, agents and producers around town.

Not always initially resorting to violence, Miranda often resorted to her own feminine wiles to land roles she was clearly unsuited for, at least talent-wise, since she couldn't act her way out of a gushing geyser. She had literally bullied her way into a "career," mostly in B movies that went straight to cable or Blu Ray, lest her upwardly mobile tactics attract more powerful attention in the higher Hollywood hierarchy. Initially she has been a porn actress, first in New York, working for her father, and later in Los Angeles. She often employed techniques from this trade behind-the-scenes, in order to land more "prestigious roles" in "legitimate" pictures that featured only soft-core sex scenes. Well-scripted stories, like Werewolf Bitches in Heat and Vampire Whores of Babylon.

Eventually, her proclivity towards promiscuity in pursuit of her professional dreams - along with her comfort in fully exposing and exploiting her own voluptuous body before the camera, any camera - resulted in Miranda Mercedes developing a cult following amongst perverts. Having grown up in New York and spending a lot of time around 42nd Street as a teenager, when it was still

Grindhouse Central, she was accustomed to this ilk. She even worked for a brief time in a peep show, just so she could torment the poor jerk-offs and laugh right in their faces. As long as they got their rocks off, her ridicule was worth the humiliation. This was how she learned to manipulate the fragile male ego to her benefit. The rest of her M.O. she picked up while witnessing first hand the many heinous acts committed in her youthful presence her father, particularly when it came to enforcing his will over others

Intimacy or intimidation, whichever worked. That was her motto. It was how she survived. And thrived.

The kneecap incidents quickly became urban legend. The bad kind. The kind that freaks people out.

The crippled redhead disappeared, presumably back to her home in a small Canadian town, crippled for life. The director, the redhead's longtime lover, was forced into therapy, both physical and mental. It didn't take. He was beyond help. But by the time he realized that, the trauma he'd suffered had become a permanent part of his damaged psyche. It was now a crucial piece of his revised identity.

# IT'S A WEIRD WINTER WONDERLAND

This event was merely the latest of dozens of atrocities committed in the notorious name of Miranda Mercedes. Atrocities that were never reported to authorities, and only shared surreptitiously via the inside Hollywood grapevine. Still, enough was enough, finally, given the particularly vicious way these latest victims were brutalized. Obviously a few bruises were no longer enough. The violence had escalated to an intolerable level, even by L.A. standards.

Miranda was ultimately blacklisted from every single casting call in the city, even from Z grade productions. The timing couldn't be worse from her point of view, since she was planning to segue into even more respectable, higher profile films, spring-boarding off her ten-year resume, however illicitly she had accumulated her questionable credits. She could only pass for twenty-five for so long, even with the regular cosmetic touchups. At least her tits were still real, and perky, unlike many aging actresses in her social circles. But even those still-succulent if imperceptibly and, with age, inevitably sagging mounds of feminine flesh couldn't help her get a foot in the door anymore.

Even her father couldn't help her, not since the indictment of his whole crew by a crusading new district attorney in league with the flag-fucking

F.B.I. They were estranged by now, anyway, ever since she refused to suck his cock when she was fourteen. He never really forgave her for that. Though she forgave him. As long as the cash and protection kept flowing, even if it was all an indirect apology for his incestuous advances. She'd take it.

One thing that experience taught her: You never know what's lurking just around that corner. Could be your own father with his boxers around his ankles and his cock in your face.

As it turned out, her destiny did suddenly pop up and poke her in the eye, but in a way she actually liked, if not quite expected. Sometimes it's the little, good things you don't see coming, not just the big, bad things.

Following the kneecap incident, Miranda's agent – who was also a West Coast Mob lawyer, not coincidentally, though he wasn't directly handling her father's defense – finally called her with an audition, for which she had been personally requested.

# IT'S A WEIRD WINTER WONDERLAND

It was for a modern remake of the 1954 holiday classic White Christmas starring Bing Crosby. Or so it was assumed, since the audition consisted of two actresses performing a duet from the movie, "Sisters," originally sung by Rosemary Clooney and Vera-Ellen. Whoever the fuck they were.

"I've never even seen that stupid fucking movie," Miranda said, lying in bed, hung-over, beside a hunk of male whose name escaped her, but whose bodily essence had dried on her thighs and lips overnight.

"Doesn't matter, the remake will probably be modernized," said her agent, whose name was Sid Stein. He was nearly eighty years old, but his vitality was matchless. His Mob connections were well known, but never discussed. Within the industry he was infamous, often referred to as "Horse Head" with a mixture of awe and fear, which is exactly what he wanted.

"I can't even sing," Miranda said drowsily. "Plus I never even heard of that stupid song." Or rather, she'd done her best to block out the vanilla sound of it.

"You can't act either," Sid reminded her.

"Just call Bruno," Miranda yawned. The hunk beside her stirred restlessly, aroused by the conversation, and then continued snoring. She got up with her cell phone and paced in the nude, groggy and sticky, after lighting a cigarette, which she smoked as she headed into the kitchen to make coffee. It was then she realized she wasn't even in her own house.

"I keep telling you, Bruno is back in Brooklyn," Sid said. "Your father put the kibosh on all that shit, remember? He's about to suffer the trial of his life. I doubt our people can save him this time, the Feds have too much on him. He will probably be indicted unless certain deals can be made, and, well, some other stuff buried."

"Maybe I should just go see him," she said, opening cabinets, looking for coffee grounds. She found some cocaine and sniffed that instead. Same effect as caffeine, only better.

"No, he's in custody. You won't be allowed anywhere near him. Just wait. We're working as hard as we can behind the scenes. Your best bet is to continue making him proud, and the best way to do that is to take opportunities as they arise, so to speak."

"Who's making it? Can I just blow somebody?"

"Your reputation precedes you everywhere, sweetheart. Even those lethal lips of yours. Nobody trusts you won't just bite it off. We can't do it that way anymore, but this is straight up. And the director asked for you specifically. He's a big fan of yours."

"You're kidding."

"No, actually, I'm not. I got this from the director myself. He just called me, in fact."

"What's his name?"

"Nobody you'd know. In fact, nobody I know. He didn't even tell me his name. He just gave me the address of the audition at a warehouse down in Santa Monica."

"Okay, what the fuck, Sid? In our business that's commonly known as a 'set-up.'"

"Oh, grow up, will you? Nobody wants to knock you off, sweetheart. Besides, I had this guy vetted already."

"I thought you didn't even know his name?"

"He thinks I don't. But he must know that I know everybody in this town, and those I don't know, get known quick if I so choose. And I so chose. He's clean, and he's good. This is his first project, and it's for a major studio, according to my sources. All I can tell you is he's just going by the name 'Billy' for now."

"What the fuck is he, twelve? What else has he done?"

"Does it matter? You don't even need to learn the song. You'll do it cold, karaoke style. He already thinks you're ideal for his vision of the role, though again, he wouldn't be specific. The project has the green light, whatever the hell it is, and these days, when you see a green light, you hit the gas and keep going, doesn't matter who gets run down in the intersection. This is a very exclusive offer, sweetheart, and you're a shoo-in. This will make you not only completely legit, but popular again, and with the right people. People that matter. Oscar-winners, festival judges, critics, self-important asshole gatekeepers like that. This is the best thing that could possibly happen to you, trust me. Just be at the address I texted you today at two."

"In the afternoon?"

"If I meant two in the morning, that would be a set-up," Sid said with a laugh.

Miranda glanced up at the starburst-shaped clock on the wall and groaned. It was nearly noon. The house resembled a midcentury modern showroom. Whoever she fucked was obviously rich. She had a type, after all. Then she saw his picture on a wall, and felt nauseous. He was a hunk of meat all right, but he had a face that looked like a pockmarked baboon. And now his simian semen was all over her. She decided to stop drinking and just stick to drugs from now on.

# IT'S A WEIRD WINTER WONDERLAND

Then she looked outside and realized she was in Palm Springs. She had two hours to get back to L.A. She threw on her flimsy leopard pattern dress and snake-skinned high-heeled pumps, then began liberally applying lipstick and makeup as she ran outside to her Ferrari parked on the curb. Her hair looked like a fright wig but many men found that just-got-out-of-bed look sexy, since it looked like she'd just had several orgasms before passing out cold. And that was almost always the case.

She hoped this director would find her messy hair a turn-on, too. It would save them both a lot of trouble.

The warehouse was on Pico Boulevard, part of an independent film studio that had long since folded. Now it was rented out for private parties and porn shoots. That's why the floor was so sticky.

Miranda cautiously entered the warehouse – which resembled an airport hangar, only smaller – after parking in the otherwise empty lot next to it. Her footsteps echoed within the cavernous confines of the hollow space. There was literally nothing inside except two chairs, one of which was occupied by a buxom young blonde whom Miranda immediately recognized, but only acknowledged with a glare and a nod. The tension between them was palpable. They had not been expecting to see each other here, or anywhere, at least anytime soon, since they both went out of their way to avoid each other, given their common history.

In front of the two chairs was a MacBook sitting open on a small table. The "Sisters" scene from White Christmas was playing on a loop.

Miranda sat down tentatively and was startled by an omniscient voice emanating from somewhere, seemingly everywhere. Actually it came from a microphone located in a booth above the room. A dark male figure was obviously at the controls, but he remained mostly hidden from their view.

"What the fuck is this, a James Bond movie?" Miranda shouted.

"Please, Miss Mercedes. Remained seated. All will be revealed. I simply want you to read the lyrics now scrolling across that screen."

Apparently the MacBook was remotely rigged to respond to his controls up in the booth. The

"Sisters" scene had indeed been replaced with a karaoke scroll.

"You take the Rosemary part, Miss Mercedes. Miss Garson, you take the Vera-Ellen part."

"Fuck this, I'm outta here," Miranda said, rising to leave.

"You will become a global star if you are cast in this role," the voice said. "Trust me. I have the connections, but they must remain anonymous for now, for reasons I cannot divulge. You have been personally selected by the director to audition for this part. Your call."

Miranda sat back down, and they both began rotely reciting the song lyrics in a monotonous tone that implied a melody without actually employing one. The other actress at least attempted to stay in tune, which wasn't hard, given the limited range of her half-assed vocal efforts. Miranda didn't even bother. She just wanted to get this over with as quickly as possible. She was just going through the motions, even if all that was moving were her tonsils.

As she musically mouthed the lyrics, Miranda was actually dwelling on her secret history with her would-be co-star, a history that would have an adverse affect on their alleged future together, in any capacity, if forced to actuate.

Despite these distracting preoccupations, Miranda had a job to do, and she did it, without any passion whatsoever. She was a professional, after all. Now that she knew exactly what the part was, and who might be her co-star, she didn't even want it anymore. Or so she told herself.

---

"Congratulations, you got the part!" Sid told her the next morning.

"Yeah, yeah, no surprise, since it was just me and that slutty bitch that showed up, and he needs two bitches to sing that stupid song. I never even met the fucking guy. He stayed up in this booth the whole time while we just read the lyrics off a computer. I didn't even sing 'em, since, as you well know, I can't fucking sing."

"Doesn't matter, sweetheart. That's how auditions work sometimes. The director just needs to confirm his own instincts. Or hers. Basically you got the organic quality he needs."

"Desperation?"

"Sure! Whatever works. The other girl had already been cast, actually. He just wanted to get a sense of your chemistry with her on film. I've seen the audition tape. It's marvelous!"

## IT'S A WEIRD WINTER WONDERLAND

"What the fuck is going on here, Sid? And that other god damn bitch hates me, and I fucking hate her right back! Her name is Greta. I used to run into her at auditions all the time. She avoided me like the plague. I don't think we can work together, Sid, I honestly don't. That mystery director needs his god damn stupid head examined. Or better yet, bashed in."

"He wants to meet you both up at a possible location in Big Bear this weekend. A cabin. It just snowed up there, so it'll be bee-yootiful."

"Aw shit, Sid. Way the hell up in the mountains? Nobody shoots out in the fucking sticks, it's cold and it sucks!"

"You do if you need lots of snow for your backdrop! I guess he's moving the action from Vermont to California. The song 'White Christmas' was actually written in L.A. during a heat wave, since the guy who wrote it, Irving Berlin, was nostalgic for his childhood winters. Did you know that?"

"Didn't know, still don't give a festive fuck. I don't want to go all the way up there."

"C'mon, it's great. They shot that old B-movie 'The Werewolf' up there, years ago."

"You mean the one where the dude goes to London 'n' shit?"

"I said it was shot around Big Bear, not Big Ben. Never mind. Just be at the address I just texted you tomorrow night by six…"

Driving up the barren highway into the remote mountains, which had only recently been cleared for travel, Miranda noticed only one other car on the road. The blonde hair of the driver convinced her it was her co-star, Greta Garson.

Greta and her had once been lovers, until they got called for the same audition. Rather than have Bruno scare her off, Miranda didn't even show up for the audition. She actually liked Greta, or having sex with her anyway. They even experienced a tinge of nostalgic lust at the audition, but otherwise didn't speak to one another. Miranda was still bitter, and Greta was still gloating.

Because of that one audition, and the fact Greta was cast in a movie that turned out to be an award-winning indie sensation, Greta became a sought after actress, a big success, dating big name directors and movie stars, her pictures in all the magazines, while Miranda was left toiling in relative obscurity.

## IT'S A WEIRD WINTER WONDERLAND

Now Greta was going to share a screen with her, only she'd probably get top billing, since she was the box office draw, if only by default. No way did she deserve that.

"No. Fucking. Way."

Miranda sped up as the two cars were approaching a sharp curve on a steep cliff, then she rammed the bumper and the other car went flying over the edge, crashing and burning into the forests far, far below.

"Now you'll be a legend, like James Dean, you dead fucking whore!"

A few miles further, her GPS confirmed she'd arrived at her destination. The snow-laden cabin looked like something out of an idyllic postcard. Too good to be true. Like most things in life.

The door was open so she just walked in. Nobody answered her knock, anyway. This was already looking bad. A shrink once told her she was paranoid. She responded by seducing and fucking him in his office during a "session, then beating the shit out of him with a stapler from his desk as he lay on the floor, weakened by his powerful orgasm and caught off guard. She never admitted she was wrong, even when she knew she was. That was against her personal policy. But something told her right from the beginning this whole thing was some kind of scam or scheme. She accepted it as a challenge. It was one more way to assert her prowess in a cutthroat industry. Word would get around some clown tried to take advantage of her, and she made him regret it. Then he gave her the part anyway. In any event, she'd come out on top. Her favorite position.

Inside the cabin it was very dark except for the dim glow of a single light bulb dangling from the ceiling in the center of the room, as well as a Christmas tree that was decorated with those old-fashioned big light bulbs, the kind that often caused fires back in the day.

A shadowy silhouette stood in the far corner of the room. The flames from the fireplace barely illuminated his presence. Miranda quickly surveyed the situation as panic began gripping her heart. The single room was sparsely furnished except for a bed in the corner, and a poorly stocked kitchenette. There was also a tiny bathroom. Beside the fireplace was a wooden walking cane leaning against the bricks, just like in the final scene of Miracle on 34th Street, one of the few holidays movies she'd actually seen, since it was father's favorite. The smoky aroma from the burning logs would've conveyed seasonal coziness if the rest of the place wasn't so desolate and creepy.

"It's me, Billy," whispered the shadow. "Sit in that rocking chair. Please. Let's get started." She noticed a digital camera perched on a tri-pod next to the rocking chair.

"Um, shouldn't we wait for the other actress?" Miranda asked, her voice quivering. The one that just died in a tragic car accident...

"What other actress? Didn't Sid tell you? I'm hiring you for both parts. I told the other girl I didn't need her after all. She was only there to sing the song with you. It was a formality since I already knew you were the one I wanted. You see, I'm recasting you in both Lynne Griffin's and Margot Kidder's roles. They were in my favorite scenes, you see. Death scenes."

Miranda took a moment to process the fact she had run a completely innocent stranger off a cliff, simply for resembling her true target. Then she snapped back to the present, since what was done was done. Even though she was wealthy, she could never afford a conscience, since it too often came at the expense of her ambitions. And where the fuck was Greta, anyway? A no-show? Did she pussy out when she discovered the identity of her co-star? Fuck it. She'd worry about that later. The current situation required her immediate attention. That's how she rolled. That's how she survived. By dealing with shit as it happened, not the way she wanted it to be. She was a realist. A sociopath, but a practical one. "Who? Sorry, I thought we were supposed to be George Clooney's aunt and some other stupid fucking bitch I never heard of who did that stupid fucking number in that stupid fucking movie."

"Just sit in the chair. Please." His voice was eerily calm and barely audible, an octave above a whisper, but still disarmingly intense

That's when Miranda noticed a one-sheet poster on the wall, for a movie she'd never even heard of, depicting a woman in a chair with a plastic bag tied tightly around her head.

She screamed and ran for the door, but he blocked her, and hit her once, dazing her enough so she was limp when he dragged her to the chair and tied her to it.

Before she could scream again, her head was ensnared in a large, heavy-duty, clear plastic bag. Despite her hysterical struggling, Billy tightened it around her throat until she passed out, then he carried her to the rickety bed across the room where he stripped her nude, except for the plastic around her head, and strapped her to the posts. He mumbled the word "Agnes" as he suckled her nipples, and then again as he climaxed on her warm belly, tenderly massaging the fluids into her supple skin. Normally when a guy came all over tasty body, she felt like a gourmet pie being adorned with some choice whipped cream. Now she felt like she was on the wrong end of a busted sewer pipe.

When she regained consciousness a few moments later, he was still straddling her with his pants down around his ankles, except now he was holding a huge butcher knife with both hands, poised to penetrate her torso. Additionally, he was wearing a red wig, framing his vaguely familiar face in long, wavy locks.

Mercedes' screams were muffled by the plastic, which also obscured her vision somewhat. But not enough to avoid the impending horror of her own brutal murder.

"You're right, I am remaking a classic holiday movie," Billy said in a surprisingly calm, steady voice. "But you got the color wrong. You see, I'm not remaking 'White Christmas.' I'm recreating my favorite scenes from my own favorite holiday movie... 'Black Christmas.' It was made in 1974 by the man who later directed 'A Christmas Story,' Bob Clark. Isn't that ironic? He inspired me to become a filmmaker myself. And I tried, I tried so very hard, but I failed. Now I make movies just for me. It's my favorite movie ever. My sister and I watched it every Christmas, even after our parents died. After we killed them. She was the only woman I ever loved. The only woman I ever made love to. None of the men I loved could compete with her, so I killed them too. They were poor substitutes, anyway. I could never love a woman the way I loved her. We moved to California five years ago, to escape the past and have a future together here, but...it didn't work out. Now nothing matters anymore. Nothing except this film. My masterpiece. I am going to upload it to the Internet and millions will see it! It is better than the original, because it's all real. It's a tribute to my late sister, who finally killed herself because of the terrible shame, which some would say I caused her, but which I know you inflicted upon her, by crippling her beauty and dreams. And now, wherever she is, we will watch it together, again and again. But you also inspired it, you see, so you should star in it. It will make you famous."

Though the thick plastic obscured his visage, Miranda suddenly recognized him, and how she knew him. But it was too late.

His eyes widened into a cold, evil stare that sliced through her flesh and into her soul, if she had one, chilling her to the bone, because they reflected her fate. Then with a discordant cry of rage and relief, he plunged the knife repeatedly into her chest as she gasped for breath then coughed up blood inside the plastic bag still tied around her neck. Once again, she was drenched in bodily fluids. Except this time, they were her own.

Her sad, sordid life passed quickly before her bulging eyes, like a bad movie on worn-out VHS tape being fast-forwarded to the good parts. Except this was the best part. Not for her, but for anyone watching. Like God. Who was probably laughing like Hell while jerking off.

While she bled to death, Billy was on his computer, typing an email: Dear Sid: Our contract has been completed. She is gone. Now she is mine. Your worries are over. There will be no dead body to link her to you, or to me. I will fuck it, then eat it, then shit it out and flush it. Please leave the money in the warehouse. You thought you knew me, but you don't. You don't want to know me, trust me. If you cross me, I will send the records of our correspondence to the authorities. This will be our final communication. Goodbye for now. Unless you fuck up. Then it will be goodbye forever.

The very last image Miranda (barely) saw as her life leaked out of her onto the cold mattress was a one sheet on the wall for Brian De Palma's first hit movie, Sisters, from 1973, starring Margot Kidder as a model suffering from split personalities, one of which happens to be homicidal.

# A Vampire, a Burglar, and an Aging Hippie Walk Into a Mall

Scott S. Phillips

"We've gotta get the hell out of here."

Pete Tyler had not been Christmas shopping since 1972 – largely because he was bitten by a vampire in October 1973, and after that, all the holiday stuff normal people worried about no longer seemed much of a concern. But not too long ago, he went and met Angie Burnett, the bartender at Hollywood dive bar the Starbucket, and everything changed.

Now Pete stood frozen in the monolithic eight-story monstrosity known as The Beverly Center, a vast shopping mecca at the intersection of La Cienega and Beverly Boulevards, skirting the

# IT'S A WEIRD WINTER WONDERLAND

edges of West Hollywood and Beverly Hills – and with only two shopping days left before Christmas, the place was a raging madhouse of elbows and oversized shopping bags, danger lurking in every direction. He felt miserably out of place with his 70s-era sideburns, white-guy 'fro, jeans, t-shirt and the frayed denim jacket covered in patches featuring band logos (all circa 1960s and 1970s, of course) and ancient slogans like Keep on Truckin' and Make Love, Not War.

"We're barely off the escalator," Randy said.

Randy "Serious" Burns, burglar and would-be stand-up comic, had offered to aid Pete in his quest to find a few nice gifts for Angie, along with Stannar Day, the 60-something-ish hippie Pete had met when the goddamn greasy magic slithered into his life in the form of Angie's deadbeat dad. Randy's shaggy blonde hair and lean physique made him look like a surfer, although he was too scared of the ocean to dip a toe in. He wore a lightweight black jacket and jeans, while Stannar sported his usual Hawaiian shirt, faded and shredding jeans, and Huarache sandals, his friendly eyes ringed by a mop of long gray hair and a magnificently scruffy gray beard. The three of them did not, to put it mildly, fit in well at the Beverly Center.

Pete stared wide-eyed at the frenzied consumers as they shoved their way through the packed mall. "It's the most horrifying thing I've ever seen."

A frighteningly thin supermodel-type shouldered Stannar aside, not even looking back to see what kind of damage she might have done. "I'm with Pete on this one," Stannar said, rubbing his man-boob where the supermodel's skeletal shoulder bone had impacted.

"There's gotta be someplace else we can shop," Pete said. "Someplace without so many people. Or any people."

Randy shrugged. "Christmas in L.A., man. It involves people."

"Yeah, but there has to be an unpopular mall somewhere."

"I'm tellin' ya," Randy said, "we should just swing by Arturo's, check out what Sexface has in the back room."

"Sexface?" Stannar asked.

"He's got a funny look on his face all the time," Randy explained.

Jostled by a pair of surly teenage girls, Pete rebounded off the glass front of a clothing boutique with an unpronounceable name. "I don't know if it counts as thoughtful or Christmassy to give Angie a stolen present."

"But it wouldn't be stolen to you –" Randy dodged a trio of Armenian men swathed in heavy cologne – "because you'd be buying it from Sexface, who bought the items from his suppliers."

"Who stole them," Pete said.

"Well, yeah, but that means the stealing is two steps removed by the time you give whatever it is to Angie."

"I don't think that takes the stolen off."

"Prices are good, though," Randy said.

A passel of screeching children nearly knocked Pete over. "Let's fuck off outta this place immediately, I can't handle it."

"Where are we gonna go?" Randy asked. "I mean, pretty much any mall is gonna be just like this."

"They make free-standing stores that are out in the world – let's find some of those that look promising," Pete said. "The stores in this place don't seem like Angie's speed, anyway."

Stannar fingered his beard thoughtfully. "Burbank. We need to go to Burbank."

"That's all the way the hell away from here," Randy said. "What's in Burbank?"

But Pete was already racing for the down escalator.

In putting on his left boot, Steve Crouch kicked the pizza box off the table, sending his dinner across the living room – and of course the box lid flew open, allowing the last few slices to land cheese-side down (of course) on the filthy carpet of his Hollywood apartment. Swearing, he collected and inspected each slice, deciding to go ahead and eat the bastards anyway. He'd eaten worse, after all.

Sitting back down on the couch, Steve took a vengeful bite of one of the now-slightly furry pieces of pizza, chewing petulantly as he glared at his tiny apartment, daring it to be even shittier than it was. It was a one-room number with tiny kitchen area that mostly went unused, although somehow seemed to always be full of dirty dishes. A closet-sized bathroom was the only other thing that could be called a room, unless you counted the actual closet, which was just about big enough to hold a broom. Steve was equally tiny, topping out at about five-one when he had shoes on, his limbs death-camp skinny while his belly protruded over his crotch, creating a pronounced dickie-do.

Little Stevie Crotch, that's what his friends called him when he was a kid, and they used to kick little Stevie in his crotch every chance they got.

Friends. Whatever.

Steve took another bite, a stringy bit of cheese and sloppy sausage dropping onto his beard where it lay on the table. Fuck. What a night. Tossing the pizza down, he snatched up his beard and went to the kitchen for a paper towel. He was afraid to get the beard wet – it seemed cheap enough that it might disintegrate – so he opted for a dry wipe, managing to do a swell job of smearing the cheese and sauce deeper into the fake gray hair.

Fuck.

Steve tried arranging the hair with his fingers, see if he couldn't hide the streak of orange-red sauce and lumpy cheese. No luck. Screw it – any kid complains, he'd just tell 'em sorry brat, but there went your Christmas. Don't agitate the Santa, man.

Returning to the living room, Steve tossed the beard down again, then put on the other boot, this time being careful not to upset what remained of his dinner. Then he slipped into the big red coat to match his big red stupid pants and shoved the rest of a slice in his mouth, chewing as he hooked the beard over his ears. The long gray wig followed. After one more bite of pizza, Steve slapped the red hat with the puffy dingleberry on his head to top off the whole shebang.

Stepping into the tiny bathroom, he checked out what he could fit of himself into the mirror over the disgusting sink. Whatever, man.

One more pause at the table to grab another bite of pizza and he was out the door, the traffic noise of Hollywood Boulevard just a block south raising a dull roar. Shutting the door, he paused to pick one more time at the cheese in his beard. Hell, any luck at all, he wouldn't even run into any kids on this outing. He had other things in mind than listening to some snot-nosed yard ape whine about what Santa should bring him, anyway. Any luck, this year Little Stevie Crotch was gonna get what he wanted for Christmas. His grin hidden within the shaggy, cheese-smeared beard, Steve set off for the stairs.

Stannar's pale blue 1972 Volvo 145 rolled along West Magnolia Boulevard in Burbank, Stannar bent over the wheel, Pete in the shotgun seat. Traffic was fairly light, given the season.

Randy, in the backseat, suddenly leaned forward, head swiveling side to side. "Isn't Master O'Cakes around here somewhere?"

"Other direction, Stannar said. "That's North Hollywood – we're in Burbank."

"I'm just sayin', maybe some pancakes would help get us in the right frame of mind," Randy said.

Pete frowned at him. "For Christmas shopping?"

Randy flopped back against the seat. "Pancakes help everything."

"What would really help," Stannar said, "is if you knew what you were looking for."

"I'll know it when I see it," Pete said. "You guys gotta give me a break – I haven't done this in a lot of years."

"Did you ask Angie if there's something special she might like?"

"Yeah," Pete said. "She wanted me to bite her."

"Bite her?" Randy leaned forward again. "Like, make her a vampire, bite her?"

"Yup."

Randy made a face. "You're not gonna do that, are you?"

"Turning my human girlfriend into a vampire for Christmas seems less Christmassy than stolen goods," Pete said.

Satisfied with that, Randy sat back once again.

Pete was authentically scared shitless about the whole Christmas shopping scenario. He loved Angie to death (but not to undeath, mind you, which is why he refused to fulfill her request for a li'l bite) and felt like he knew her pretty darn well even though they'd only been together for a handful of months, but going out and trying to find something specific, something just for her, something that she would love? Man, that was a lot of pressure for a guy who hadn't done this sort of thing in so very, very long. What if he picked something out and it just wasn't her bag? He knew she'd fake it pretty well, but he didn't want her to have to fake it – he wanted to get her something she'd really like, even if it was just goofy and simple.

"Maybe we can get pancakes after," Randy said.

"You and your pancakes," Stannar said. "How does a guy who eats so damn many pancakes and waffles stay so thin?"

"I am blessed with the metabolism of a mongoose."

# IT'S A WEIRD WINTER WONDERLAND

"Hey hey —" Pete pointed at something up ahead. "What's that place? I've heard Carmella mention it."

Stannar squinted into the night, trying to figure out what Pete was gesturing at. "Where?"

"Dark Delicacies," Pete said. "Find a parking spot, let's go in there."

"No spaces out front," Stannar said. "Let's just park on a side street."

"Shit," Randy said.

"What now?" Pete said.

"Just try to park where we don't have to cross any streets," Randy said. "I got a thing about crossing streets."

As the car passed Dark Delicacies, Randy stared at the Frankenstein's monster mannequin standing outside, a Santa hat perched jauntily on his blocky head. "This place doesn't seem any more Christmassy than getting bit by a vampire."

"Frankenstein's wearing a Santa hat," Pete said. "That's Christmassy as hell."

Stannar turned right onto North Avon Street. "You two are Christmassy as hell. Let's get this show on the road so I can get home and go to bed."

"Cheesebeard!" the prissy little pigtailed girl screeched at Steve, wriggling away from him.

"Rosie!" the little girl's equally-prissy mother scolded. "Don't use that language."

"But he has beard cheese," Rosie said, pointing. "He's a hobo."

"A ho-ho-hobo," Steve said.

"Yuck." The little girl tore loose of her mother's grip and scurried off down the sidewalk.

"Rosie!" Mom made a pouty face at Steve. "I'm sorry."

Steve shrugged, his cheesebeard rising with his shoulders. "No big deal."

He watched as prissy mom pursued prissy daughter, finally catching up to her at the corner when the little girl had the sense, much to Steve's surprise (and chagrin), to stop before running out into traffic. Mom waved at Steve while the little girl stuck her tongue out, then they both crossed the street, sadly not getting run over in the process. Once they were a reasonable distance away, Steve pulled the woman's wallet from his oversized Santa pocket and checked the contents. Mostly credit cards he'd be afraid to use – he'd

## IT'S A WEIRD WINTER WONDERLAND

never been much of a stolen credit card guy, it seemed too easy to get caught – and twenty-three dollars in cash. Considering the boutique store the woman and her little girl had come out of, she had to be using her cards and not cash. The cash was probably earmarked for a refreshing post-shopping stop at Romancing the Bean or something. Damn it – not even worth the trouble to lift it from her purse. Pocketing the cash, Steve tossed the wallet onto the sidewalk just outside the door of the store the woman had exited. Let somebody else find it, play Good Samaritan, and wind up taking the blame for lifting the bread.

Twenty-three bucks. That was all he had for his troubles so far, standing around in the ridiculous Santa outfit, needing to pee. He'd started out hitting the Burbank Town Center, the sprawling collection of stores, restaurants and megaplex cinema just up Magnolia Boulevard, but cut out of there after about a half-hour. Too many goddamn Santa's at the malls, all of 'em looking far more Santa-like with their clean red suits and cheeseless beards, while Steve looked exactly like what the prissy little girl had called him – a hobo. He'd cut out of the Town Center and made his way down the road to this little stretch of fancy boutiques and oddball shops, figuring maybe he'd stroll the sidewalks for an hour, see what he could come up with.

Shit though – maybe he wouldn't have to stroll around. Maybe find himself a little plastic bucket, something like those Salvation Army people use, just pick a good spot and stand there, ring a little bell or whatever, let people drop their money in the bucket of their own free will. Ain't even really stealing, is it?

Stuffing a hand in his pocket, Steve fingered the twenty-three bucks and looked around at the various stores. None of the fancy clothing joints were gonna have what he needed, but that shop up the street on the other side of the road, the one with Frankenstein standing out front – that looked like some kinda devil store, definitely a place that might sell little plastic witch's cauldrons or something. He didn't much like the look of the trio of oddballs heading towards the store, but hey – he was a legitimate customer, right? Just a dime store Santa looking for a little bucket.

As he hustled across the street, Steve kept a wary eye on that Frankenstein, making sure it wasn't a real dude in an outfit begging for change. Last thing he needed was more goddamn competition.

# IT'S A WEIRD WINTER WONDERLAND

Having found a parking space that did not require Randy to face his fears, the three determined shoppers made their way towards Dark Delicacies, dodging a few other folks along the way.

Randy eyed Stannar's battered old Huarache sandals slap-slapping the pavement. "Don't your feet get cold? Your toes are right out there in the world."

Stannar's fluffy beard parted in a satisfied grin. "I've got California feet."

Randy seemed dubious. "I don't know, man. I don't like my toes exposed."

"Toes are part of nature," Stannar said. "They should be allowed to enjoy it instead of being cooped up in boots all the time."

"Maybe not so much the week before Christmas, though," Randy suggested.

"To each his own, my brother."

Pete eyed Frankenstein's monster as they walked past the creature. "I gotta say, I was a little concerned that this thing was gonna turn out to be a guy in a costume waiting to jump at us."

Stannar pulled the door open, holding it for Pete and Randy. "You two both need to mellow out."

"Whatever, George Berger," Pete said.

"Who's George Berger?"

"From Hair, man. I woulda thought you'd have it memorized."

Stannar followed them in, letting the door swing shut. "Think about the time period during which I would have seen Hair and consider why I might not remember anything – other than the naked girls."

"Point taken," Pete said.

The trio paused just inside the shop, taking it all in. The place was long and narrow, floor carpeted in green and the walls painted the color of dried blood. Bookshelves lined one wall, glass cases on the opposite side. A few tables, clothing racks and other displays were scattered here and there throughout the store. The counter and register sat not quite halfway down on the right side, an older fellow tucked behind it, a mad cluster of long white hair surrounding his friendly face and equally-white mustache and goatee. In his black t-shirt and black jeans, his pale head and arms appeared to be floating. At the moment, there were only a couple other customers, browsing the books near the back of the store, which suited Pete just fine.

As for the store's wares, Pete immediately understood why Carmella — owner of the popular Goth nightspot Club Emoglobin down on the Sunset Strip (and also a vampire) — liked the joint so much; the shelves were lined with horror books, books about horror, and all manner of creepy and unsettling other things. One rack held nothing but horror movies on DVD. There were horror-related toys and action figures and lunchboxes, and the clothing racks held all manner of Goth-y clothing. Even the jewelry and perfume was horror-themed. He wasn't quite sure he'd find something for Angie in the store, however — she did indeed seem to harbor a love for a particular vampire, but had never expressed much interest in the horror genre outside of her boyfriend's bloodsucking affiliation. Still, though — the place was jammed to the rafters with cool stuff, and Pete felt remarkably comfortable in the store, unlike the stores at the mall — or nearly any other store anywhere, for that matter.

"Can I help you guys find something?" the man with the white hair asked.

"We're, uh, looking for girlfriend presents," Pete said. "But no idea what, exactly."

"We've got lots of girlfriend presents." The man made a sweeping gesture to indicate the vastness of the store's supply of girlfriend presents. "Take a look around and let me know if I can help."

"Thanks." Without a clue where to start, Pete wandered off towards the nearest rack of clothing, Stannar and Randy sticking close to him. Pete eyed the two men. "Maybe we oughta split up."

"Why?" Randy asked. "We know even less what we're looking for than you do."

Sighing, Pete began flipping through the clothes on the rack.

The man with the white hair watched Pete and the others for a moment. "You guys really are lost, aren't you?"

"'Fraid so," Pete agreed.

Stepping out from behind the counter, the man approached the befuddled shoppers. "Is there a particular monster or movie or author she likes?"

Pete looked to the others for guidance, found none. "Well," he said, "she digs vampires, I guess."

"You guess," Stannar sneered.

Pete glanced toward the door as it swung open and a rather crusty-looking Santa Claus strolled in, making eye contact with Pete and quickly averting his gaze. The man with the white hair greeted

## IT'S A WEIRD WINTER WONDERLAND

Santa, who grunted softly in response before heading deeper into the store.

"If she's into vampires, maybe she'd like this." The man with the white hair led Pete and the others to a nearby table, where a weathered wooden box with a hinged lid and worn carrying handle sat. As the man lifted the lid, Stannar – a bit ahead of Pete – suddenly fired an open palm into Pete's slightly-tubby belly, stopping him in his tracks.

"Whoof," Pete said, shooting a confused look at Stannar.

Stannar said nothing but wobbled his head around in a variety of ways, apparently suggesting Pete hang back.

"This is nice gift for anyone who's into vampires," the man said. "It's a vampire-slaying kit."

Finally understanding why Stannar gave him the shot to the gut, Pete took a couple steps back.

"You guys look it over – I'm gonna see if Santa needs any help. Gimme a shout if you need anything." The man with the white hair strolled away towards the crusty Santa.

"Big ol' crucifix in there," Stannar told Pete.

"Yikes," Pete said. "What else is in there?"

Randy peered into the wooden box. "The usual – couple of stakes, a mallet, bottle of holy water, a little mirror." He looked at Pete. "Does this seem kind of offensive to you?"

"Why?"

"Just that this guy is selling something designed expressly to kill you."

"Well, it's not really designed to kill me personally," Pete said. "Just vampires in general. And judging from everything in this store, my guess is, this guy knew he had a real vampire shopping in here, he'd be overjoyed."

Stannar shut the lid on the box. "For safety's sake."

The three continued browsing. Pete hoped like hell that something would jump out at him and shriek I AM FOR ANGIE, but he could feel his stress level rising.

"No, no, I need a little bucket. Liiittttle."

Pete glanced over to see crusty Santa making a little bowl of his hands to show the man with the white hair what he was looking for.

"But not too little, y'understand?" Santa explained. "People need room to make those donations for the underprivileged."

# IT'S A WEIRD WINTER WONDERLAND

"Sorry," the man with the white hair said. "All we've got is the big cauldron. It'd hold a lot of donations, though."

"But Santa can't carry it so well, can he?" Santa said. "And sometimes Santa needs to make haste."

"I can give you a shopping bag, if that would help," the man said. "People could drop donations in that."

Santa considered for a second. "Yeah, fuck it, let's do that."

Pete noticed Randy eying Santa warily as the jolly old elf followed the man with the white hair back to the counter. "That guy's gonna pull something."

"Why do you say that?" Pete asked.

"Remember where I've spent a significant portion of my life, the kinda guys I've associated with," Randy said. "I know the look."

Stannar nudged Pete. "Let's get into position."

"For what," Pete said. "You wanna jump him?"

"If we have to," Stannar said.

"He might have a gun tucked into that Santa suit."

"Yeah," Randy said. "He definitely looks like the sort."

Pete and the others hung back where they were, watching anxiously as the man with the white hair reached under the counter, coming up with a large plastic shopping bag sporting the store's logo. "Here ya go, I hope this helps."

Santa took the bag, sizing it up. "I believe it will." He opened the bag, holding it towards the man. "Now, how 'bout you drop a donation in there."

"Told ya," Randy whispered.

"I could start you off with a couple bucks," the man said.

"I had something more substantial in mind," Santa said. "The contents of the register."

The man with the white hair cocked an eyebrow at Santa.

Santa smiled and waggled the bag. "For the underprivileged."

The man with the white hair, maintaining that cocked eyebrow, simply stared at Santa.

"Fill it up," Santa repeated. "Or I'll fill it up."

Giving in, the man with the white hair opened the register with an embittered cha-ching and began pulling cash from the drawer.

"We've gotta do something," Pete said.

"Uh-uh." Randy nodded towards the frightened customers at the back of the store. "Three of us plus those two — I can assure you, a guy who'd rob a place with five customers inside is either crazy as a shithouse rat or doesn't have any problem killing someone who might try to be a hero."

Pete frowned. He didn't like it one damn bit, but figured Randy knew what he was talking about. He watched angrily as the man with the white hair dropped the last of the cash into the plastic bag and made a sour face at Santa.

Santa waggled the sack again. "Go on and put the change in there, too."

The man did as he was told. Smiling, Santa spun the bag, twisting the top closed. With a smug grin, he bolted for the door and ran out.

"Come on," Pete said, running for the door. "We can at least see what he's driving, try to get the license number." Pete dashed out onto the sidewalk and skidded to a halt, Randy and Stannar nearly slamming into him.

Santa seemed to be in no hurry – not running, just walking at a fair clip down the sidewalk, no more than fifteen feet or so from Dark Delicacies.

"Hey, asshole!" Pete hollered.

Santa stopped, not looking back.

"Oh shit," Randy said.

"I thought we were just gonna get his license number," Stannar said.

"Yeah, I kinda just blurted out that hey, asshole," Pete said.

Santa whirled, snarling, his face contorting, teeth extending into fangs. Unleashing a furious growl, Santa twisted and cracked and popped as he transformed, brown-black fur sprouting on his hands and face, fingernails becoming claws, face elongating into a furred snout, the cheese-encrusted Santa beard dangling beneath slavering jaws.

"What the fuck now is this?" Pete said.

"I think he's a werewolf," Randy said.

"Come on, werewolf," Pete said. "My ass."

Stannar, eyes glued to the snarling beast in the Santa suit, quietly said "You know, for a vampire, you sure seem to have a hard time buying the existence of other such creatures."

The Santa-wolf took a threatening step towards Pete and the others, his Santa boots slopping loosely around his thin wolf legs and paws. "You guys had best just fuck off," the werewolf said, voice guttural.

"It talks," Stannar said.

"And bites." The Santa-wolf clamped its jaws together with an unpleasant snap.

Pete was glad to see there were only a few shoppers strolling the sidewalks, most of them too far away to get much of an inkling of what was happening with Santa. "How do you stop a werewolf?" he whispered.

"Silver bullets," Randy said.

"That would also require a gun," Pete pointed out. "How else?"

"No clue," Randy said.

Pete glanced at Stannar, who shrugged.

Getting an idea, Pete darted back towards Dark Delicacies, yanking the door open to find the man with the white hair on the phone, apparently to the cops. "Got anything silver in here?"

"Actual silver?" the man asked, hand over the phone's receiver. "What for?"

"Actual," Pete said, "and don't ask."

Stretching the long cord on the phone, the man ran across the store to the vampire-slaying kit and flipped the lid open. Grabbing something, he spun towards Pete. "Here, but I want it back!"

Pete's eyes widened as the man with the white hair tossed the crucifix to him.

Unable to fight the deeply ingrained catch-whatever-someone-throws-at-you instinct, Pete snagged the cross out of the air in both hands. Holding down the urge to shriek in agony as the crucifix seared into his flesh, Pete instead banged back out the door, immediately tossing the cross to Stannar. "God DAMN that HURTS!" Pete squealed.

"I thought I told you to get lost." Annoyed, the Santa-wolf started towards Pete and the others, stumbling a bit on the loose boots. Pausing, the werewolf kicked the boots off, then, with a raging (but slightly embarrassed) growl, the monster bared its teeth and came at them again.

"Run like hell," Pete suggested. As they took off, Pete caught a glimpse of the man with the white hair, his back to them, still on the phone, completely unaware of what was occurring outside his store.

"I guess this explains why he didn't pull a gun," Randy said.

Pete cut hard around the corner of the building, Stannar hopping through the turn, while Randy cut it too sharp and banged off the wall before tripping over Pete, who had come to a stop with his back against the wall. Randy face-planted into the sidewalk, skidding a couple feet on his chin.

"Fuck," Randy muttered.

Stannar ran on a few more feet before realizing the other two were no longer running. "We're stopping now? Why are we stopping?"

"I'm about to do something stupid," Pete said. "Throw me the cross."

## IT'S A WEIRD WINTER WONDERLAND

At that instant, the Santa-werewolf leapt around the corner like a cat-scare in a cheap horror movie, growling and slobbering, lips pulled back from gnarly teeth. The Santa hat still rested atop its head, bushy wolf-ears poking out from beneath the ring of white fur at the base of the hat.

"Now!" Pete shouted.

Stannar threw him the crucifix. Pete nearly missed the catch, partly out of anticipation of the scorching pain he was about to experience. After bobbling the cross for a moment, he gripped it tightly, brandishing it towards the werewolf even as smoke began to rise from his crisping skin.

The werewolf sneered. "Crosses don't work on werewolves, asswipe."

Pete lunged at the werewolf, bringing the crucifix down hard to stab the monster in its shaggy shoulder at the base of its neck. The wolf let out a piercing howl of agony, dropping the sack of money and clawing wildly at Pete, spinning around in an effort to dislodge him. Pete held on tight, shoving the cross deeper into the wound, then released his grip on the monster, scrambling out of range of its flailing claws.

The werewolf staggered for a few steps, then fell forward onto Randy, who let out a little shriek of his own. Whimpering and twitching, the werewolf shifted back into human form and lay there groaning, the crucifix still jutting from his shoulder. Blood ran into his Santa beard, which had wound up around his neck like a hairy gray kerchief.

Randy wriggled from beneath the scrawny dude and got to his feet, gingerly feeling his scraped chin. "Ow."

Stannar walked up to stand next to Randy and Pete. "Should we leave that thing stuck in him, y'think?"

"I guess," Pete said. "I don't know how werewolves work."

Santa peered up at the trio, sniffling a little. "It's Christmas, you dickheads."

---

Pete, Stannar and Randy walked back into Dark Delicacies, dragging the bleeding Santa along with them, the cross embedded in his flesh. "Got him," Pete told the man with the white hair.

"Jeez," the man said. "You think we oughta pull that thing out?"

"Maybe let the cops do it — could be an artery thing," Pete said.

## IT'S A WEIRD WINTER WONDERLAND

The man made an ah yes, an artery thing face. "At least the Santa suit kinda hides the blood."

Stannar handed the sack of money to the man with the white hair, who peeked inside. "Merry Christmas," Stannar said.

The man grinned wide. "Maybe you guys oughta pick out some girlfriend presents – it's on the house."

Pete's anxiety over having chosen the wrong present grew exponentially right up until the moment on Christmas Eve that he and Angie went out onto the deck overlooking Hollywood to exchange gifts. The house was a large Spanish Colonial tucked away in the Hollywood Hills, not far from the famous Hollywood sign, and had been left to Pete (for some sinister purpose he hadn't figured out yet, he was certain) by Carson Fitzgerald, the vampire who had turned him all those years ago. Although terrified of the house, Pete had recently moved into the place along with Angie and Carmella and the other Club Emoglobin vampires, Pinball and Elric. Pinball had gone to Hilray Hobb's apartment in North Hollywood for the night, while Carmella and Elric were up in

Carmella's room enjoying a Bob Clark double-feature of Black Christmas and A Christmas Story.

Angie, long blond hair whipped by the slight breeze, pulled her coat around herself and smiled at Pete, the smile that always killed him.

"I hope you like what I got you." Pete looked at the awkwardly-wrapped package he held. "As with so many other things – ahem – I'm totally out of practice with Christmas shopping."

"I dunno, you handled the ahem part pretty damn good right outta the gate." Taking Pete's hand, Angie looked out at the lights of the city. "And anyway, this is a pretty good present right here." She reached into her coat pocket and tugged out an envelope bound up in a bow. "Here ya go, foxy."

Grinning, Pete took the envelope, handing Angie her gift. "I also don't know how to wrap shit good."

"It's cute, it's like a little kid did it." She gave him a look of anticipation. "Ready?"

"You first."

Angie tore back the wrapping paper, a smile spreading across her face. "Are these jammies?"

Pete nodded. "I know you like to sleep all naked and whatnot, but since we're living here with all these vampires, I thought you might like something comfy to wear for roaming around the house."

Angie unfurled the pajamas. "They've got little vampires on 'em!" Wrapping her arms around Pete, she squeezed him tight. "Thank you, sweet baby – I love 'em."

"Really?"

She released her grip on Pete and stepped back. "Yeah. They're all soft and snuggly." She pointed at the envelope. "Now you."

Feeling a bit undeserving, Pete slipped the bow off the envelope and slid a finger under the flap. Puzzled, he removed the contents and peered at them. After a second, his eyes went wide. "Are these actual Woodstock tickets?"

"Yup," Angie said. "All three days."

"Holy cats – where did you find these?"

"I got 'em from an old hippie who bought tickets for the show, then couldn't make the trip because he got busted for possession. He's had the things ever since."

"Stannar?"

"Believe it or not, this was a different old hippie."

Pete couldn't believe what he held in his hands He'd seen a lot of shows in his time, but Woodstock was one he had missed. "Dang – I'm gettin' kinda misty-eyed here." He looked into Angie's big blue eyes. "Thank you so much."

"I've never had a fella fight a werewolf to get me a Christmas present before," Angie said.

"Believe me," Pete said, "that was easier than dealing with the mall."

# Riven
## Sarah L. Johnson

**I'm** over here.

No, not there by the chip bowl with sergeant flop sweat and his military brush cut, button down, buttoned all the way up, his every third Pyrex invasion a double dip.

Jesus.

Over *here*.

Good. Now you see me, the girl in the corner throwing serious shade your way. You're late. The party is in full holiday swing. Deck the halls and all that shit. You put in some mirror time this evening, I can tell. Your beard is trimmed, shiny, and submissive, but still you, and it works. But him...with a brush cut you can see the scalp and it looks unhealthy. Nothing to corral the perspiration coasting along cranial sutures onto his ruched forehead. That's some concentration. Double dipping focus. Don't look, don't look.

He saw us looking. See what you did? Now I have to go over there and say something that makes him feel special about himself, like I haven't noticed the soggy plaid shirt and a bowl of contaminated dip. It's his regimented body language that interests me. A way of carrying that chip from dip to mouth to dip that means war. Failure is not an option.

No, no, you stay. You've done your part, exceeded your reach. I'll take it from here, and congratulations on making yet another social situation more awkward for me than it is for you.

I walk away, leaving you to your bewilderment. It's Christmas Eve. A special night. Why am I being such a snot? Like more than usual? I could tell you it's complicated but complicated is what people say when the truth is too simple, and ugly, and no one wants to fucking hear it.

You're more into me than I'm into you.

In terms of absolute measurement, I can't argue, but my ability to feel is better measured on a relative scale, like humidity. I may not have a ton of love floating around inside, but I'm so chilly that even a small amount fogs my windows. You get it? I don't have as much love as you do, but where you're sitting at about 80% saturation, I'm raining inside.

I wander over, grab a chip out of the bowl, and hold it up to the light. "Ever seen Jesus in the ripples?"

His pale-lashed eyelids twitch. "Pardon?"

Who the hell fastens the top button of their shirt when they aren't wearing a tie? You must feel what I'm thinking because your proud smirk dips in and out of my periphery and the rain pours down.

Brushcut shakes his head and a glob of dip falls from his chip, plopping on the carpet between his sneakers. Laces frayed and straggling. No way is he Army. But that top button…he might have a weird relationship with his mom. I know, I know, it's not that huge a deal, just buttons, you'd say, but even you don't believe that. Deep down everyone knows it's the little things that make you want to kill someone. I ask about the army anyway because dudes like it when people mistake them for a soldier.

"I'm not," he admits. "But I play one on TV."

"Actor?"

"Call of Duty…a video game…that I play on the TV…"

## IT'S A WEIRD WINTER WONDERLAND

This is just awful. Silence swells in the closed space around us and I drill a burr hole before we're both crushed under the pressure.

"Cool," I spit the word like a gout of bad blood.

It isn't cool. Or hot. It's tepid. A mild 19 degrees on the thermometer of human intrigue. Water you can drink without feeling it. So boring it ought to be illegal, but otherwise he's not extraordinary. Sixty-five percent H2O, a homeostasis every skin job at this house party maintains despite attempting to flush their vascular systems with the second-cheapest wine.

Your eyes are still on me, still asking what kind of bean I've got up my ass tonight, and I'm getting to it, okay?

Once again the answer is both simple and hideous: he's not the usual.

Brushcut may be an emotional eater, but he's no drinker. Like me, he's sober and present, and thirst is a terrible thing. Really though, it's because he double dips, dresses like Norman Bates, and can't be arsed to tie his shoes. It's that goddamn top button, and you're watching me, watching so closely. You've seen this before, and I wish you'd look away now.

"Your antler is drooping." Brushcut points to my left breast where the antler sewn on my sweater has flopped down to obscure a large loamy eye. "Kinda gives Rudolph a saucy come hither look."

I cross my arms over my chest. "Don't sexualize my reindeer."

"Sorry." He blushes to the roots of his bristled hair.

"They're majestic creatures."

His head bobs, eager to agree and perhaps trickle his way into my good graces. You offer a slight nod of your own. Christ in the manger, you really know how to pick them. We're doing well tonight.

"I was going for festive," I blurt out. "But every girl here is in a cocktail dress."

Brushcut shrugs. "Ugly sweaters are a Christmas tradition."

"So are uncomfortable office gift exchanges, weight gain, and mulled wine with racist grandparents."

"Don't forget Santa."

I blow my bangs out of my eyes. "That's just a story."

"Gotta be a reason we keep pretending, right?"

Brushcut's grin reveals a snaggletooth I find charming even if he smells like an onion. Must be the holiday spirit.

## IT'S A WEIRD WINTER WONDERLAND

Sensing the shift in my mood, you stroke your tidy beard. You can tell I like him and you're proud of your choice. Well, fuck you. Don't be so smug. You smell like cookies and taste like brown sugar and I dig you more deeply than I thought I was capable of, which still isn't much by any normal person's standards...but just don't, okay? You're distracting me.

From what I'm trying to build.

From tradition.

Rituals we perform over and over because during this most magical time of year, we're not alone. You, me, Brushcut, and all those who came before. We're vulnerable. We're connected.

"Earth to Rudolph," Brushcut snaps his fingers in front of my face and I consider biting them off. They'd taste like minced garlic and mayonnaise. However, I've been a moderate asshole so I can forgive him. And he's comfortable enough to tease me. Brushcut has a backbone. He's worthy. When his eyes lock over my shoulder I know he's looking right at you. "That your boyfriend?"

"Nope." I toss you a dismissive glance. "Friend-ish. Sort of a father figure. It's complicated."

Brushcut is confused. Anyone would be. Confusion is good. Curiosity, even better.

"Did you know deer could be carnivorous?" I ask.

"No way."

"Google *doe eats baby bird*. Happens now and then. Zoologists and animal behavior experts have theories, but no one really knows why."

"Rudolph the saber-toothed Reindeer."

I point to my sweater. "This isn't Rudolph."

"He's got a red nose."

"Reindeer are the only female deer species that grow big antlers."

"You seem well informed."

"There's a lot we can learn from them."

"So you're like, Jane Deer." He breaks up laughing, though his joke isn't nearly as charming as his fucked up teeth.

"My friends call me Riven."

He squints. "Ribbon?"

"Are you fucking retarded?"

"You're a scary girl."

I sigh and rub my temples. "I'm trying to tell you a story."

"About Rudolph?"

"The red-nosed retread. Disney fairytale version."

## IT'S A WEIRD WINTER WONDERLAND

"I suppose the real story is far more Grimm?" He leans in, chips forgotten, a blot of dip on his chin. "Tell me."

"You know Dasher and Dancer and—"

"Prancer and *Vixennnn*..." he sings out the names.

"Don't," I snap. "Truth is, the most famous reindeer of all didn't have a name. Not back then. She didn't need one. She was wind and darkness, ice and instinct. No reindeer has ever been as swift in the sky or as sure on the shingles. She led, only because she couldn't follow. Klaus loved her above all others. She was his Magdalene."

Brushcut pulls a face. "You mean he...with a reindeer?"

"It's a metaphor, you twat." I grab a napkin and scour the dip from his chin. "His companion, his equal, and like good ol' Mags, she got erased while he went on to stratospheric fame."

"What happened to her?"

I casually scan the room. You're mingling, surrounded by a herd of cocktail dress girls. You've got time to kill.

"It was the clearest Christmas Eve anyone could remember," I say. "Sky stretching out endlessly under a crescent moon. She couldn't help flying the team faster and higher, too high, and the sickle of the moon slit her belly. They landed the sleigh on the nearest rooftop where she slipped her torn harness and fell to the ground. The clatter from above woke the gentleman of the house. He threw back the curtain, lifted the sash, and leaned out to find her bleeding into the new fallen snow. She wobbled to her feet, a broken antler hanging over one wondering eye. Enchanted, the man reached out and touched her nose. But she was so thirsty you see, from blood loss.

"By the time Klaus and his coursers got down from the roof, she'd ripped the guy's throat open. They found him hanging out the window, draining into the snow and her lapping up the puddle."

"Did she survive?"

He's asking questions. There's a brain under those bristles, a heart under the fastened buttons. I blitz the room again, but I don't see you. You've had enough of spectating like a perv. Maybe you've gone outside to smoke your pipe, you hipster motherfucker. You'll be back. I'm only here because of you.

"I hate parties," I say, suddenly exhausted and hot as hellfire in my sweater. "So loud. Want to go somewhere quiet?"

His chip pauses between his lips. "Alone?"

"No, dipshit. I was thinking we'd take the whole party I hate with us."

He's wounded again until I hop on the table, skirt sliding up my parted thighs. I grab a plastic cup and gulp a few swallows of rummy eggnog, all the while burning him down with what you call my doe eyes. He drops his chip back in the bowl, goddammit, and you return, stamping snow from your boots, just in time to watch me take Brushcut's sweaty hand and lead him down the dark hallway.

This isn't me, but in the moment I pretend I'm that girl. Get drunk way too early, flash my gash at strangers. A part of you wishes I were That Girl. Vivacious. Sexual. A part of me wishes I could be That Girl for you. Another part wishes you knew I'm never closer to being her than when I'm with you. Again, it's all relative. I pull Brushcut inside the first bedroom I find and shut the door on the twinkling din.

A whole raft of cocktail dress girls rent this house, so I'm not surprised to find an open closet puking up a glut of scarves, skirts, tunics, and jeggings. Likewise, the top of the dresser is strewn with cosmetics, chewing gum, and baubles. A string of pearls hangs around the neck of a ceramic winged cherub holding a bow and arrow aimed right at the unmade bed. I turn the little monster around to face the wall. Its naked ass blushes in the snowy light.

I ease onto the bed and bury my face in the sheets, inhaling that elusive funk great perfumers fiend for. Top notes of lavender and newborn babies underscored by a foulness we can't help wanting to roll in. Dirty hair, oily skin, sweat, shit, sex. Worse than pigs. This filth is what makes us human.

The mattress dips as Brushcut follows me onto the bed. If he's surprised I'm not immediately diving for his dick, he doesn't show it. In fact it doesn't seem to occur to him at all as we lay on our sides, facing each other, not touching, his broad forehead lustrous as a pearl.

"This is better," I say.

"If parties aren't your thing, why'd you come?"

"Tradition."

"Even if you hate it?"

I rip my eyes from the sour neck flesh straining at his buttoned collar. Sleet ticks against the windows, painting the room with blurry blue shadows. Brushcut understands my thirst for connection. It's why you chose him. It's why he came.

"Every year, over and over," I say.

Brushcut shakes a fist. "The power of Christmas compels you."

"Okay, you need to stop."

"Thought girls liked funny guys."

"I feel like I'm in bed with my dad."

"And that's weird."

"Well, it's not fucking normal." I grind the heels of my hands into my eyes. "Just be quiet. Makes it easier for me to barely tolerate you."

His face crumples. "Jeez...you're really mean, you know that?"

"Then why are you still here?" I ask, I plead. *Go, just go, leave me alone, please*... But they never do.

His fingers worry a pinch of gamey sheet between us. "Tell me the rest of the story?"

Eyes shut, he listens through the dark, waiting for my voice, and I love him a little. Just a little. Of course you want me to like him, but this, I'm sure, would surprise you.

"She survived," I say. "She ate and slept and carried on. Spent most of her time alone, which wasn't unusual. But her wound never healed, and when Christmas got close again...well, she went nutcrackers, bashing her head into the stable walls, biting at the other does. Klaus had two choices. Put her down, or pay the price to treat her condition."

"What did he do?"

"Had his PR machine pull off an epic rebranding. Turned himself into Santa Claus, a fat jolly elf with a new team lead he made sure became the most famous reindeer of all. Rudolph the Red Nose."

"That's one heck of a story."

The windowpane rattles and naked poplar branches whip and sway in the gale. It's the night before Christmas and the chill I've kept at bay all year nibbles at the edges of my calm. Molars grinding, I manage not to shiver but can't do anything about the icy sweat greasing every inch of my body.

"You okay?" His big dumb hand bounces off my shoulder and tumbles into the ditch of my waist. Unbelievable. My sweater creeps up and his fingertips skitter over a stripe of bare skin. This happens. They all touch me sooner or later. A normal girl might show him what to do, where to go, how to heat up his lukewarm moves. But I'm frozen, wet and cold, a block of melting ice in a nest of dirty sheets.

The touch. You explained it to me once. They get lost in the narrative and the touch is how they reach back into reality. You say it hasn't got anything to do with sex. As if that makes me more comfortable.

"So she's still out there?" he asks.

"Yeah, with a slit open belly and a snout dripping blood. Klaus gave her what she needed in secret, but Santa threw her under the runners of history's sled."

"His Magdalene."

"The lady vanishes."

Brushcut's blown pupils brighten with the ecstasy of understanding as he continues to stroke that slippery slice of skin at my waist. True, it doesn't feel sexual. It's more intimate than that. More real. You wouldn't understand. It's the part of this situation you can't reach into, though I've never told you as much. I want you to be comfortable.

I push him away when he attempts to trace along the edge of my skirt over my stomach.

"Sorry, I'm sorry." He retreats, jamming his hand roughly underneath him as though it ought to be punished.

He wants me to tell him it's okay, that it's me, not him. But it's so him. He did everything wrong. Double dipping. Egregious sweating. Dad jokes. A prissy slob with his top button and untied laces. Worst of all, he fell in love. With the story. Not at first sight, but at first sound, which is less common, but doesn't negate the fact that falling is by far the dumbest way to find yourself in love.

The tap of snow against the window ceases and the moon razors through the clouds. I cock my head towards the door.

"What?" he asks.

"It's quiet out there."

"Not a creature was stirring…"

"Don't be an asshole." I prop myself up on an elbow. "Think the party's over and they forgot about us?"

"Maybe they thought we were taking a long winter's nap."

"That what the kids are calling it these days?" I can't help laughing a little, just a little.

His jackstraw grin collapses. "Not sure what the kids would call this."

Already he's climbing off the bed. He wants to go. He's had enough. He's had nothing. I reach out as he crosses the room, opens the door and slips into the hallway. *Wait…please stay…* The words don't come. I don't want them badly enough. Before I follow, I turn the disgusting cherub and his little arrow back to face the bed.

## IT'S A WEIRD WINTER WONDERLAND

As we prowl down the hall towards the living room, Brushcut's hand tightens around mine. "Where is everyone?"

I stare up at him. Doe eyes. At first I didn't know what you meant by that. Doe eyes. I likened it to something gentle, warm, something nothing like me. You knew better. *Google it*, you said.

In the living room the curtains are thrown open. Moonlight pours over eight women standing in a semi-circle, silent and unmoving, matching reindeer sweaters pulled over their cocktail dresses.

Brushcut empties his lungs in an onion dip gust and tugs at his still-buttoned collar. "What are they doing?"

"They live here," I say, drawing him into the semi-circle. Then I pull my sweater over my head, woolen fibres sliding through the sheen of perspiration. My skin itches and crawls under the wide strip of gauze taped to my stomach. The front door opens, and a draft drills up my spine and into my brain.

You.

Crisp and trim in your red shirt, snowflakes melting on your oiled beard. The sweater girls flock to you, all eager gazes and hushed chanting.

*Merry Christmas to all, and to all a good night.*

*Merry Christmas to all, and to all a good night*
*Merry Christmas to all, and to all a good night...*

Gentling them, you pat their necks and pop a sugar cube into each pretty pink mouth – Blitzen, Dancer, Comet, and Vixen – all of them. Then you take my hand and rein me in. I wince as you work a fingernail under the edge of the gauze and peel it away from an incision running from my sternum to navel. I screamed the first year you cut me. I scream every year. Because I can't cry, anymore than a reindeer can. Because I run too cold, too fast, too high. My inner life is my only life, I lead because I can't follow, and the moment you set eyes on me, you saw her.

Brushcut guppies a few times, then speaks. "It's just a story."

*Duh*, I think, but choose my words carefully in front of you and the sweater girls. "Truth and facts aren't the same. Truth goes deeper."

"Too deep." He gestures to the horror of my sliced open self.

"It's tradition."

I'm surprised when he slaps you with an accusatory glare. "You did this to her?"

His concern is touching. I regret not being more generous. Like a bored hand job would have killed me? As if I'd spoken the thought aloud, you sweep my hair aside and kiss the chilled sweat behind my ear. So much for comfort. You're caught up in the narrative, same as Brushcut, except your touch has everything to do with sex and you don't care about reality. You never have. I admire that. I envy it.

"Why?" Brushcut asks, like he doesn't already know. I understand the compulsion to complicate what's simple. It's easier to drink the ugly truth from the lips of another.

The sweater girls fidget, a giddy shine in their eyes. Brushcut turns so pale you'd think he was the one cut open. All I want is to see that messy smile, and hear him laugh in spite of himself. I can't look anymore. Your beard scratches my naked shoulder as I burrow into your arms, into the sweet dry heat of you.

In many ways I'm more connected to Brushcut. We have a deeper reach into the situation. No one believes in Santa, yet year after year they act out the same fiction. Your pageant is no different. Brushcut and I don't need to believe to feel the same thirst, to bleed for it.

More rapid than eagles, the sweater girls surround us. I pull the knife from your belt, a slender crescent of steel. Typically, you do this part – it's tradition after all – but you lay a finger alongside your nose and nod. Cupid giggles as she and Prancer clutch Brushcut's arms. With a flick of my wrist, that top button is history.

# Ho Ho Ho

Brent Nichols

A̲mhurst.

A shitty little town in the middle of a shitty frozen prairie. It sucked in the summer, with half-wit redneck farmers driving their pickup trucks up and down Highway 36 and pretending they were going somewhere, with mobs of yelling kids too young and stupid to know this miserable hole would put a stamp of backwards yokel ignorance on them they'd carry for the rest of their wasted lives.

But at least in the summer you could go outside, put a little distance between yourself and the drawling knuckle-draggers. In the winter the town got as cold as Carol's eyes the last time she looked at me, as cold as that empty place inside me where I used to carry my dreams of something better. In the winter everyone stayed inside. Which meant I spent every waking hour either alone in my roach-infested shithole of an apartment or cooped up with my fellow citizens.

Bad enough when it was the mall or some crap restaurant full of dickheads in baseball caps. It was much, much worse when you found yourself cooped up in a funeral home.

I showed up early, too. Not out of respect for Mrs. Marley, the guest of honour in the box up front. More from a perverse sense that I was going to show her she was wrong about me. I didn't impress her much as a kid, and her opinion deteriorated when I grew up. She wouldn't expect me to turn up for her funeral, and she sure wouldn't think I'd be on time.

A quick glance left and right showed no mourners in earshot. I muttered, "Christmas Eve in a blizzard. And I'm twenty minutes early, you old bitch."

Cloth rustled behind me. It was the only warning I got before a thick hand smacked into the side of my head. I let out a yelp and saw every head in the room swivel toward me as I twisted around in my seat. "What the hell?"

The elderly lady sitting directly behind me laid a glare on me that shrivelled my balls in my scrotum. She was a big woman, but that's like saying Amhurst lacks culture. It's what you call a gross understatement, with extra gross. She was a behemoth, damn near five feet wide. How she ever managed to sneak in behind me I'd never know. I should have heard floorboards creaking. Hell, I should have heard groans from the sidewalk outside.

"You keep your foul mouth shut for the rest of the service, Ben," she hissed. She lifted a fist that looked like a loaf of pink bread with inset dimples for knuckles. "I'm not afraid to box your ears."

*I'd like to box your head*, I thought, *as in cut it off and put it in a box*. I'd been terrified of Mrs. Kozinski since I was seventeen and in love with her daughter. I settled for giving her a dirty look.

"Now, don't sulk." Her voice was softer now, but the threat was still there, just under the surface. "It's a funeral."

*I know it's a funeral, you old buzzard*. I didn't speak the thought aloud. She hadn't lowered her fist, after all. I glowered and started to turn away.

And froze. If Mrs. Kozinski was here …

I turned back, telling myself not to, telling myself to *be cool, it doesn't even matter if she's here, if she is then the best way to play it is to ignore her, don't even look*. But my head kept turning anyway, story of my life, know it's stupid and do it anyway. It took quite a while to turn that far – Mrs. Kozinski was a large woman, as I mentioned – but at last I was twisted sideways in my seat with my head cranked around well past two hundred and seventy degrees, and then I just stopped breathing for a while.

There she was. Life-size and real and so much better than the fading image I'd been carrying around in my head for ten years. Carol Kozinski, the girl who moved right into my brain and set up house and had been living there ever since, as much a part of me as my spleen even though I hadn't seen her since I was twenty years old.

The blonde hair was shorter now, the green eyes colder and staring right through me like I was furniture. I wanted to say ... something, anything, I just had no idea what. I got as far as opening my mouth but I knew by the look on her face it wouldn't do me any good.

She looked older. That was a shock. I mean, I knew a decade would leave a mark, but still, to actually see tiny wrinkles around those hypnotic eyes .... I wanted her to be fat and homely and married because then I might have been able to let go. She wasn't, though. Ten years had added a mantle of maturity and confidence to the impossibly pretty girl I was still in love with. I looked at her and knew I'd never be free.

Another face smirked at me from beyond Carol's shoulder. Just as blonde, just as pretty but without that air of sad wisdom, face a bit more round but so much like a younger Carol that my heart lurched in my chest. I might have spent another minute staring with my mouth open if Mrs. Kozinski's fist hadn't moved in my peripheral vision.

I straightened around and fixed my gaze on the front of the room.

The younger girl had to be Christine. Baby Christine, who was proud and excited to be starting school, clutching a Disney backpack and hurrying to the school bus the last time I saw her. That made her, what? Sixteen now?

The same age Christine was when I broke her heart.

The doors opened behind me and I felt cold air touch the back of my neck. I didn't turn at the sound of feet stamping snow from boots, but a murmur moved through the sparse crowd, and I saw heads turning or leaning close to other heads to whisper. It could only mean one thing.

Mrs. Marley's only son Jake was here.

# IT'S A WEIRD WINTER WONDERLAND

It was close on three years since I'd seen Jake, my best friend since before I even knew Carol existed. I stared at his mother's coffin until Jake himself appeared in the corner of my eye. He wore an ugly red jumpsuit and a white government-issue parka with CORRECTIVE SERVICES stencilled across the back and snow dusting the shoulders. He had a goon on either side of him, and he clanked as he moved. He couldn't take his coat off because his hands were cuffed in front of him. He moved to a seat, shuffling awkwardly, a foot and a half of chain linking his ankles. He paused long enough to sneer at everyone who was staring at him, and then he sat down, a minder on either side.

I watched him for a moment longer, feeling a familiar churn of conflicting emotions. Then I went back to staring at the coffin.

The service was interminable. I was there because Mrs. Marley had been almost kind to me, or if not kind, had been a fixture in my life during my childhood. But the saccharine eulogy and the endless clichés didn't mesh with my memories of the stern woman I'd known and occasionally feared. So I looked out the side window and watched the falling snow and waited for the whole grim farce to end.

It was snowing like it was never going to stop, like God finally noticed what He'd created here and decided in His infinite embarrassment to blot it from the Earth with ten or fifteen feet of frozen, remorseful tears. Not that a snow apocalypse would work. Rednecks are as hard to kill as cockroaches. They might be racist, drug-addled, pig-shit-scented thugs who thought the giant mall in Edmonton was the pinnacle of Western civilization, but they were practical. If it snowed for forty days and forty nights they'd pop out of the snow banks on the forty-first day, raring to restock their liquor cabinets and buy more of my drugs.

And I, God help me, would still be here to sell to them.

Once, I'd held Carol in my arms and whispered into her hair about how I'd leave, and take her with me. I'd be so gone from this place, and I'd never come back. I remembered the certainty I'd felt back then, the absolute knowledge that I was leaving and no power on God's Earth could stop me.

Then came a giddy, breathless phone call from Jake. He'd been selling drugs full-time for a year by then, running himself ragged seven days a week and making less than I made part-time in the town's one and only Seven-Eleven. All that was about to change, though.

The RCMP had made a massive bust in Lloydminster. They seized pot and cocaine, and they arrested nine key members of a gang that had been funnelling drugs from Toronto to rural Alberta.

"Bullshit," Jake assured me. "Not a gang. Just a bunch of assholes who sort of worked together. And now they're all busted. And you know what that means?"

"You have to get a job?" I said.

He punched me on the shoulder. "No, assface. It means that opportunity is knocking." He punched me again. "Feel it knocking?"

"I feel a dickhead knocking," I said, and punched him back.

"This is our chance." He backed out of range and gave me that crazy grin of his, the one that meant life was about to get interesting, the one that got me suspended three times and finally expelled a month before I would have graduated from High School. "We's about to become players!"

We argued for two solid hours, and at the end of it I spent two solid days driving him to Winnipeg. He tracked down a friend of a friend, a mid-level entrepreneur who'd survived the big bust and was wondering how he was supposed to unload half a million dollars' worth of Mexican weed and Columbia's finest snow.

I hung back and did my best to look tough and Jake did what he did best, dishing out a banquet of bullshit about all the contacts he had and how much product he could move. And it worked, and at the time I even thought that was a good thing.

We were going to be rich. This was the big leagues, and the serious bucks were just around the corner. So I stayed in Amhurst, and I became the biggest drug dealer in fifty miles, and I never got rich, but it was so much better than Seven-Eleven that I couldn't let it go.

Carol was unimpressed, so I swore I'd get out of the business. Sell my share to Jake, take her somewhere nice, or at least somewhere that wasn't Amhurst. And then I got high and took an alternate form of payment from a hot little number who liked to smoke a joint on the weekend. Carol walked in on us, and that, as they say, was that.

At last the whole dreary service came to an end. By the time I stood and turned, Carol and her mother were gone.

The dead woman' sister stood near the exit, and the mourners filed past her, paying their respects.

## IT'S A WEIRD WINTER WONDERLAND

No one seemed to know quite what to do about Jake. He stood at the back of the room, a burly Sherriff on each side of him, and the old women who'd come out to send off one of their own gave him doubtful looks, then circled wide around him on their way to see his aunt.

*Fuck this*, I thought. I ignored the swollen-eyed old bat and headed straight for my former best friend.

"Ben." He'd aged more in the three years since his arrest than Carol had aged in a decade, but he smiled when he said my name and the years fell away. "Thanks for coming, man."

We shook hands, his left hand coming up with his right because of the cuffs. Then he gestured toward the corner with his head. "Do you mind, guys?"

One of the goons gave a grudging nod and I followed Jake to the side of the room. We were a whole ten or eleven feet from his escort, but if we kept our voices low we'd have something not entirely unlike privacy.

"I can't take it anymore." That was his opening line. He lifted his wrists, and they trembled, making the chain tinkle. "The shackles," he said. "The locks. The bars. The people." A spasm made his face clench up like a fist. He stared at me, his face haunted. "And I've got ten more years."

There was nothing to say to that. I tried to give him a sympathetic look and wondered if I should have lined up with the old broads to see his aunt instead.

"I'm giving you up," he said.

"Huh?" I honestly didn't get it at first. Except a slow chill was climbing my spine, one vertebra at a time, so I guess I suspected.

"For Dingo," he said. "I'm doing a plea bargain." He lifted his hands, the closest he could come to a shrug with the cuffs on. "They don't really care about the drugs. They got a real hard-on for Dingo, though."

I gaped at him. We'd been arrested, together and separately, a couple of times each over the course of our careers. The cops knew who we were. But we, despite my delusions of grandeur and dreams of wealth, were small fish. We got bullshit possession raps, and they turned us loose.

Until one ugly night when a piece of shit named Domino Yasinski, known as Dingo to his associates, had ripped us off for more than a grand and then had the gall to come by asking for an eight-ball on credit. I decked him. One good shot to the mouth, broke off his left top eyetooth and cut up my knuckle. I was in the kitchen washing the cut when I heard the gunshot. My first thought was that Dingo was packing and we were finally in real trouble.

I was only half right.

"But I didn't kill Ding! You did!"

He made a shushing motion, the prick. "I know. I know. But there was no one there but you and me. And if I say you did it, well ...." He did that shrug thing again and gave me a weak grin. "I can't stay inside, man. I'm sorry. I just can't do it."

I stared at him, feeling sick and cold. I thought about lunging at him, strangling him right there on the floor of the funeral home before he could deliver his bullshit testimony and fuck up what was left of my life. But killing a man in front of a dozen witnesses, including a pair of cop wannabes, hardly seemed like the way to dodge a murder rap.

"I did something to make it up to you," he said. "I know it's kind of a shit deal." That was an understatement, and the look on his face said he knew it. "At least I warned you, right? Gave you a few days to get ready?"

There were no words for this level of bullshit. I settled for "Fuck ..."

"It'll be rough inside," he said. "If you get out again it'll be for a day or two, and you'll be wearing chains like mine." He rattled his cuffs. "But pussy is what you'll miss the most." He leaned toward me and gave me a conspiratorial wink. "I got you covered, though."

"For fuck's sake, Jake."

A hurt look flashed across his face. Honestly hurt, like I should be grateful for the favours he was doing me as he ruined my life. "I lined you up some pussy," he said. "You better enjoy it. It's the last you'll be getting for a long time."

"Jake, no. No, man, you can't do this."

His eyes slid away from my face. "I gotta. But, hey. Listen. The pussy." He held up three fingers. "I got you three chicks. Three, man!" He didn't quite meet my eyes as he flashed a shit-eating grin. "It's all arranged. They'll come to your place tonight."

One of the goons approached. "All right, Marley," he said. "We gotta go. The snow's getting bad out there." He took Jake by the arm and tugged him toward the door.

Jake stared at me over his shoulder. "Enjoy it, buddy! Then get your shit in order. I don't see the prosecutor until Monday. That's how long you have."

The other goon opened the door, and I shivered as a blast of snowy air blew in. "Three!" Jake called as they pulled him outside. "Don't ever say I didn't do nothing for yah!"

The door swung shut and I was alone with a dead woman and my own dark thoughts.

\#

I'm pretty sure the Imperial Arms would be condemned in a real city. Standards were low in Amhurst, for building codes along with everything else. I dug around under my coat for my keys, noticing the lock was jammed as usual and went on into the lobby. Fish was loafing on the worn-out sofa by the stairs. He perked up long enough to give me a hopeful look, his eyes telling me he was jonesing and begging me for a dime bag. I ignored him and he slumped back down.

My apartment was a rat hole. I could remember being proud of it, once. Back when it was my first apartment ever. But I still lived in the same place ten years later, and that was a sad testament to how my life had gone.

A quick search told me I was out of booze. I wasn't going back outside for more, either. The snow was more than a foot deep and still falling. I wasn't going anywhere.

There was nothing on TV but cheesy Christmas specials. I turned off the box and sat in my living room as the sun went down and the room got dark, thinking about Jake, and prison, and chains.

Could I make a run for it? I had three thousand dollars stashed in the lumpy cushions of my couch. It wouldn't get me far, not with a murder rap hanging over my head. It wouldn't get me much of a lawyer, either.

"I didn't do it," I mumbled. "Fuck." I thought about beating him to the punch. I could go to the cops, tell them everything I knew about Dingo. In fact, I could call them right now, get the whole process started. My phone lay on the old door draped across two stacks of bricks that served as my coffee table. But a cold lump of futility in my stomach kept me slouched right where I was. It was hopeless.

I was fucked.

I was still there, staring at my phone, an hour later when someone knocked on my door.

*Carol.* There was no sane reason for her to be at my door, but the image of her filled my mind. I wanted it to be her, wanted it with a sudden sharp desperate hunger. I wanted to back things up, reverse this ugly train, roll it back ten long years to that night I held her in my arms and told her about how I was leaving, and taking her with me.

It wouldn't be Carol, though.

# IT'S A WEIRD WINTER WONDERLAND

The knock came again.

"Beatrice," I muttered, and shuffled toward the door. Beatrice was my girlfriend, more or less. I wasn't too sure how long she'd hang around if I stopped sharing my inventory with her. But she smiled when she saw me, and sometimes I caught her looking at me kind of misty-eyed, like she didn't see a shitbag drug dealer at all. Like she saw that guy from ten years ago. We were going through a rough patch, but I was pretty sure she cared about me. Really cared. I would tell her about this whole mess. Maybe she could help me find a solution. At the very least, I could count on her for a bit of sympathy. I really needed some sympathy.

I opened the door, and the smile froze on my face. "Angie."

She gave me a sexy smile, but there was a hint of bitterness mixed in. "You remember my name. That's good."

I might not have managed it if I hadn't already been thinking about the past. I took a step back. "Come in."

She came in and closed the door, still smiling, but with wariness in her eyes. She was not dressed for the weather. She had a short fur coat and a mini skirt, and little boots with high heels. I said,

"It's good to see you. It's been ... ten years." I knew almost to the day how long it had been.

She took off her coat, looked around, and found the closet. She wasn't wearing a whole lot underneath it, just a lacy top with spaghetti straps that left her shoulders bare.

Her nose wrinkled, and I realized my apartment didn't exactly smell great.

"Sorry. Um, I can't really open a window."

"Not in this weather," she agreed. There was snow in her hair, glittering as it melted in the soft blonde curls that framed her face. She was a pretty girl, and I remembered why I hadn't hesitated on that awful day so long ago.

"You look good," I said.

Dimples appeared in her cheeks, and she looked me up and down. "You're not looking so bad yourself."

There was something artificial in the way she said it. "Angie? Um, I'm glad to see you. But why are you here?"

Her eyebrows arched in mock surprise, and she put all her weight on one leg, arching a hip provocatively. "I'm here to see you, big boy." She reached out and trailed her fingers down my chest.

# IT'S A WEIRD WINTER WONDERLAND

I suppose I should have liked it, but I felt suddenly ill. In the aftermath of Jake's betrayal I'd forgotten his bullshit promise. "Are you here because of Jake?"

Her coquettish smile became a bit fixed. "Yes. But never mind that." She took a step toward me, her boots clumped loudly on the floor, and she said, "Hang on a moment." She knelt awkwardly, fumbled with the boots, and stepped out of them. "That's better." She stepped right up to me, her breast touching my side and making a warm circle that spread through my body and set my heart thumping. "Do you want to show me where the bedroom is?"

I could smell rose perfume, and a hint of apples from her hair, which was just below my nose. She put both hands on my waist. The blood roared in my ears, so I naturally said the stupidest thing possible.

"You're hooking now?"

She flinched, and her hands tightened momentarily before she let go and stepped back. The smile was gone now. "What about it?"

"Nothing," I said hastily. "It's just – I mean – I didn't know." Amhurst was a small town. There were only so many people moving around in the shadows, and I knew most of them.

Her lower lip protruded, and she stopped looking pretty. "So?" There was a world of challenge in her voice, and resentful anger in her eyes.

I shrugged helplessly. "What? I'm just surprised, that's all."

"What?" She jabbed me in the chest with a hard forefinger. "Surprised I would stoop so low?" The finger jabbed again. "You think I'm too good to make easy money?" Jab. "You think I'm too good to live like you?"

I opened and closed my mouth a few times. "But I'm not a hooker."

I'm not saying there was a right thing to say, but if there was, that wasn't it. Her eyes narrowed to slits. "Oh, no, not you. Not Mr. big shot drug dealer. You don't have to spread your legs, do you?"

I edged back a half step. Her hands clenched into fists and she took a half step forward.

"You think you're the only one who wants money? You think we don't see you, hanging around in the Eddie all day, flashing a big roll?" She lifted a hand, and I flinched. There was a momentary flash of amusement in her eyes, which quickly turned to bitterness.

## IT'S A WEIRD WINTER WONDERLAND

"Maybe I saw the way you lived. Maybe I wanted to be like you. But I couldn't be the drug king of Northeast Alberta. No, you already had that sewed up." Her lips peeled back from her teeth like she was going to lunge for my throat. "So, I sold something else, okay?" Her face spasmed. "I'm a whore. Is that what you wanted to hear? I'm a whore!" She hit me then, a punch to the chest with a lot of passion behind it but no technique. "Are you happy now? I said it! I'm a whore!"

She threw another punch, staggering when I dodged. I steadied her with a hand on her shoulder, and she caught her balance, then jerked out of my grip. "Fuck you, Benny. You hear me? Fuck you!" Her eyes filled with tears and she turned away from me, fumbling blindly for her boots. I stared at her, feeling baffled and helpless, while she tried again and again to get her foot into one of her boots. She almost fell, and I turned around and retreated to my living room before I could do something stupid like try to help.

I flopped down on the end of my couch where I couldn't see her and listened while she stomped and cursed and cried. After a ridiculously long time I heard my front door swing open, then slam shut.

"Well," I said to my empty living room. "That was ... interesting." And Jake was going to send me two more of these delightful surprises?

Fuck.

Knuckles rattled against my door, a quick frenetic knock like an excited woodpecker. I called, "Go away."

"You all right in there?" It was Fish. "Everything okay?"

He sounded like a caring friend, but I'd fallen for this flavour of bullshit before. He would invite himself in, spend all of thirty seconds ingratiating himself, and then hit me up for a dime bag. I said, "I'm fine, Fish. Please go away."

"You sure, man?"

"Fuck off, Fish."

I put my feet up, the wood of the converted door cool and smooth against my heel where my sock had worn through. I sniffed the air. Angie was right. This place had a definite fug, a stink of man-sweat and sour milk. I could clean up, but the place would still be a dive.

*Maybe I wanted to be like you.* Was she nuts?

Well, yes. That seemed clear enough. Wanting to be like me, though? I was a walking cautionary tale.

# IT'S A WEIRD WINTER WONDERLAND

I dozed off thinking about booze, trying to think of a single place that might be open late on Christmas Eve. I woke with a start, a kink in my neck, my legs cold and numb, my feet still on the coffee table. I stared around the living room, disoriented. The whole scene with Jake now seemed bizarre. Could it have been a bad dream? I couldn't seriously be headed for prison.

Could I?

*Thump thump thump.*

I came to my feet, my back protesting as I uncurled it, and took four stumbling steps toward my front door before my brain caught up with me. Did I really want to answer it? I didn't think I could face another hooker.

On the other hand, the memory of Angie's breast touching my chest was fresh in my mind, blended with an older memory of when we'd gone much further. The older memory came with way too much baggage, so I pushed it away and put my eye to the peephole in the front door.

Beatrice stood in the hallway, distorted by the fisheye lens, her nose the size of a cantaloupe. A wave of emotion washed over me, stronger than I would have expected. She wasn't mad anymore, or if she was, not too mad to talk about things. I pulled the door open, stepped into the hall, and took her in my arms. She stiffened for a moment, and then her arms went around me. I felt as if I could have held her forever, but I saw motion in the corner of my eye. It was Fish, staring at me with blank eyes and an open mouth from the end of the corridor.

I drew Beatrice inside. "Babe. It's good to see you."

The smile she gave me was a little tired, but it seemed genuine enough. "You too, Ben."

"I'm sorry," I said. I helped her out of her coat. "I don't even remember what we were fighting about, but I probably started it. I know I say a lot of stupid shit." I hung her coat in the closet, immensely relieved that Angie was long gone. What if a hint of her perfume lingered? I sniffed the air.

Nope. Just bachelor fug.

I took her in my arms once again. She felt wonderful, warm and soft and fragile, and I vowed to do better by her. She deserved a man who would cherish her, protect her, and I was going to do all those things.

Except ... I was going to prison.

She broke free of my embrace and took a step back. She smiled, though.

## IT'S A WEIRD WINTER WONDERLAND

*Take it easy*, I told myself. *Don't come on too strong.* Being an idiot, I ignored my own advice, beamed like a fool, and said, "Beatrice. I'm so glad you're here."

"Um, thanks, baby. That's nice."

A sudden horrible thought loomed in my brain. Jake was sending me two more hookers. With any luck the snow would keep them away. But what if one of them showed up while Beatrice was here? "Listen," I said. "I have to tell you something. I saw Jake today."

The smile disappeared and her face sort of closed up. Jake was one of the things we sometimes fought about.

"Listen," I said, "you were right about him. About how he's a bad influence." I smiled without humour. "In fact, you're more right than you know."

She stared at me, her face blank and still.

"Anyway, I might be in a bit of trouble because of him. I'll tell you about that in a minute. First, though ...." I forced a chuckle. "He decided to do me a favour." I lifted my hands, palms out. "I did not ask for it. I never agreed. But, he .... Well, he decided to send over some hookers." I gave another fake laugh, showing my disdain for such a ridiculous idea.

Beatrice said, "I know."

I stared at her, and she stared back, her face expressionless. And all that warm emotion inside of me just drained away, like someone pulled the plug in a bathtub. And there I was, naked and cold, waiting to find out just how bad it was going to be.

"He called me," she said. "He asked me to come over."

*Asked you? You mean, like a favour? Because he knows I care about you, and he knows I'm going to need someone to talk to?* I said, "He ... asked you?"

She nodded. "He gave me two hundred dollars."

The light seemed to drain out of my apartment. I could barely see her in the darkness. I said, "But why would he ...."

"I've been doing some work on the side," she said. Her voice was cool, distant. "I thought you knew."

Instead of answering I stood there like an idiot, staring at her expressionless mannequin's face.

"I'm sorry," she said. Her voice was kind of soft and wistful now. "I thought you knew." Then she turned and slipped out of my apartment and I was alone.

# IT'S A WEIRD WINTER WONDERLAND

An hour later I was still awake, staring morosely through my living room window. The snow no longer fell. It lay deep and pristine over the streets and sidewalks outside, hiding the cracks in the pavement, giving everything the look of a bad knockoff of a Thomas Kinkade painting. No tracks disturbed the snow. Nothing moved outside, and I wondered if my third hooker would show.

I hoped not. And yet .... Here I was, two hookers in, and I hadn't even been laid yet. Swirling images filled my head, of Beatrice when I tied her up, of Angie with her shoulders bare and her breast touching me, and ten years ago when I took her on the couch in Jake's apartment.

Carol, before Angie came along and I ruined everything. Carol, with her high firm breasts and a mix of love and lust in her eyes as she reached for me.

Maybe she would be the next girl. It would fit, I supposed. It seemed like everyone in my life was hooking now. Why not Carol? The idea of it sickened me – but it was the only way I would ever be with her again. If Carol had fallen that low, well, maybe it brought her all the way down to my level.

I nodded to myself, my decision made. If another woman showed up at my door, I would nail her, no matter who it was. I closed my eyes, fantasizing, remembering Carol and the way she would slide her dress down over her shoulders one tantalizing centimetre at a time.

Headlights lit up the street outside, the glow visible through my eyelids. I opened my eyes, and a blocky SUV ground its way down the middle of the street. The snow was deep, as deep as I'd ever seen, flying up from the grill of the SUV. The big machine churned its way down the street until it was directly outside my window. It paused, and my mouth went dry.

Then, with a powerful rumble from its engine, the SUV surged ahead, the back end fishtailing for a moment before it rolled out of sight.

I slumped down on the couch, feeling a lump in the stuffing dig into my back. That was something I needed to address, and soon.

But not right now.

"Christmas is over, buddy," I muttered. "No more presents to open. You had your chance."

More headlights flashed outside. I sat up in spite of myself, then stood and walked to the window. It was a shitty little Volvo this time, rolling along in the tracks left by the SUV and still having a hard time. As the car neared my building it picked up speed, then swerved abruptly to one side. The front end ploughed into deep snow and the car came to a stop, not exactly parked at the curb, but with all four tires out of the original ruts. The door swung open, and a young woman got out.

It was her. The closest streetlight was a ways off, but I knew. It was Carol. She peered at the building, and for a moment I swore she was looking into my eyes. Then she started toward the front door, taking big, exaggerated steps in the deep snow. She wore a long, sensible coat and proper winter boots, and I smiled. Common sense wasn't supposed to be sexy, but on Carol it was.

I hurried to the door, opened it, then closed it again. I didn't want to look too desperate. But I *was* desperate, and what if she lost her nerve waiting to knock? Or saw Fish and got creeped out?

I stuck my head and shoulders into the hallway. Fish was a dozen feet away, sitting on the floor, staring vacantly at the opposite wall. "Fish!" I hissed. "Go the fuck away."

He started, banging his head on the wall behind him, and looked around, blinking. I pulled back into my apartment before he spotted me. Carol would be here any second, and I wanted to make the right impression.

The apartment was still a dive, though. I wasn't going to change that with thirty seconds of frantic tidying up. I retreated to my living room and turned in a slow circle, feeling the old futility wrap itself around me. In the end I did nothing at all. I just stood there and waited for her to knock.

The knock when it came was hesitant, timid. This was not the brassy, confident Carol that I knew. This was someone unsure of the reception she would get.

Like visiting an old boyfriend. You might be nervous – if you still cared.

I walked to the door. I felt light, like I was floating above the stained ruin of my carpet. My whole body tingled. It was like being high, but so much better. I hadn't felt this way since ...

Since the last time I was with Carol.

I opened the door.

"Hey, sailor." She smiled, opening her coat. She wore nothing but a peach-coloured bra and panty set underneath.

For a long moment I stared at her without speaking. Then I said, "Christine?"

## IT'S A WEIRD WINTER WONDERLAND

She gave me a mock pout and closed the coat. "Are you going to invite me in?"

I blurted, "You're sixteen!"

"Almost seventeen," she said. The coat opened again, just an inch or so, and my eyes moved down in spite of me. "It's all firm and unspoiled, Ben. And it's all for you."

"Oh, yeah," said Fish in the distance. "It's all for me."

Christine grimaced, pushing past me, closing the door behind her. We stood there looking at one another, and then she said, "Didn't Jake tell you I was coming?"

"He said three hookers."

"And I'm number three!" She did a little pirouette. "Surprised?" Her gaze moved down. "I can see you're happy to see me."

I untucked my T-shirt and made a completely inadequate attempt to hide the erection that was trying to tear its way out of my jeans. "Christine ..."

She stepped close to me and put a hand on my crotch. My hands went to her shoulders, and there was a terrible moment when I almost tore the coat from her shoulders.

Then I pushed her back.

She blinked at me with hurt-filled eyes. "What's the matter?"

"You're a kid," I said, wishing she would zip up the coat. "You're sixteen."

"I'm a woman. I can be your woman."

"No." It should have been an automatic reaction. Instead, the effort of speaking that one short word was like lifting a refrigerator. "I can't have sex with you. It wouldn't be right."

"It's already paid for," she said plaintively.

"And you can keep the money. Please. Do up your coat."

Christine stuck out her lower lip. "Come on, Ben. You're my first customer. I wanted my first time to be with someone like you."

"Oh my God." I took a deep breath, trying to figure out what I could possibly say without sounding like a complete hypocrite.

"It's going to happen," she said. "You might as well accept it."

"It's not going to happen." I wished I sounded more certain.

"It's inevitable," she told me. "Jake said you're going to prison. He said you'll be there for a really long time." Her tongue touched her lips. "You'll want a woman eventually. By the time I'm eighteen you'll be desperate for it. They do conjugal visits, right?" She leaned against the wall behind her, somehow making that simple movement crackle with sexuality. "But how are you going to find a woman from in there?" She shifted, and a long bare leg slid out from under the coat. "I'll come see you then. And you won't be so squeamish next time. I'll be your girl for five hundred dollars a visit."

I stared at her, my mouth dry.

"You'll fuck me like you've never fucked anyone before. It's destiny."

I grabbed the shoulder of her coat with one hand, used the other hand to open the door, and shoved her bodily into the hall. Then I slammed the door and locked it.

Virtue makes for cold company, especially when you know you haven't accomplished anything. Her transition from bright teenager full of potential to gaunt whore full of heroin would continue unchecked. She needed better examples in her life. She needed to be kept away from men like me. She needed someone to take her out of Amhurst and surround her with people who had jobs and educations and dreams and shit.

I flopped down on the couch, stared up at the water stains on the ceiling, and thought about my life. I might beat the murder rap, but it would hardly matter. Apparently I was constitutionally incapable of leaving this turd of a town. I would keep on selling drugs until I ended up locked up with Jake. And Christine would come to visit me, and I'd fuck her until my money ran out.

It was destiny.

I fell asleep, and I dreamed of Christine's funeral. The other mourners were a blur, but I saw Carol, still young, still pretty. In that bleak nightmare Christine had died in her teens of an overdose. Carol cried brokenly at the grave, then lurched away, pausing long enough to spit on my tombstone in passing. I tried to tell her that it wasn't my fault. I didn't do anything wrong, but then, I didn't do anything right, did I?

I woke with a start, my face pressed against imitation leather, a savage knot forming in the muscle just under my left ear. I stumbled to my feet, hissing with pain, digging my fingertips into the side of my neck while I tried to separate dream from reality. The sun was up, and it was a new day. My heart slammed in my chest like I'd snorted a pound of coke, and a single blazing thought illuminated every foggy corner of my overwrought brain.

It might not be too late.

I threw open my front door. Fish was asleep directly across the hall, sitting with his back against the wall. His head rose, he blinked several times, and then his eyes focused on my face.

"Fish," I said. "It's Christmas day, isn't it? Today's Christmas."

He shrugged. "I guess so."

Last night was Christmas Eve. More than a foot of snow came down yesterday afternoon, right when every plow driver wanted to be home with their families. They'd go to work if they had to, but they'd expect double time and a half. And Highway 16 would get priority. They wouldn't reach Amhurst for hours, if not days.

"He still here," I told Fish. "He's stranded by the snow."

"Huh? Who?"

I didn't answer, just reached down and hauled him to his feet. "I got a Christmas present for you, buddy." I dragged him unresisting into my apartment. His legs wobbled, and he staggered toward the couch.

"Not there." I manoeuvred him sideways and got him seated on the coffee table instead.

"Hey, man." His voice was full of wonder, like a small child after Santa has come. "This is a door."

I ignored him, finding a gap in the stitching on the couch, burrowing my way into the seat cushions. A thick wad of cash with an elastic band around it went into my hip pocket. After that I pulled out my stash. I dumped it all into Fish's lap, a brick of cocaine the size of my fist, damn near completely pure, and a Mason jar full of fentanyl.

Then I slid my hand back into the cushions, and I really dug deep. Cold springs slid across my wrist and dried-out stuffing scratched me as I burrowed into the bowels of the couch. Finally my fingers touched a solid metal shape. I got a good grip, made sure my finger was outside the trigger guard, and pulled out Jake's old Saturday Night Special.

Fish had torn a hole in the plastic wrapper on the cocaine. He was scrabbling at the brick with his nails, but he froze when he saw the gun.

I sat down, resting the pistol on my knee. It was the same gun Jake had used to shoot Dingo, and it still held five rounds. "Fish," I said, "we have to talk."

He said, "*Aaaahhhh...*"

"I've given you a present. Now you're going to give me a present."

Alarm filled his features, and his eyes flicked to my crotch.

"You're going to give me an alibi," I said patiently. "I have to go out for a little while. Later on, though, you're going to tell the police we spent the morning playing cards."

Fish said, "Cards?"

Did I even own a deck of cards? I imagined the cops grilling us separately, asking what we'd played, who won, what colour the cards were. "You're right. Stupid idea." I shoved the pistol into my waistband, grabbed the remote, and turned on the TV. "We spent the morning watching TV." I glanced at the TV, saw Bruce Willis in a wife-beater shirt, making fists in the carpet with his toes. "We watched Die Hard. I was here the whole time."

Fish nodded absently, his gaze returning to the cocaine.

"Fish?" I waited until I had his attention, tapping a fingernail against the butt of the pistol. "Don't fuck this up when the time comes. People who rat on me come to a bad end. Understand?"

For a moment there was actual clarity in his eyes. "I understand."

"Good man. Don't overdose, okay?" I bundled up, transferred the gun to a coat pocket, and grabbed a balaclava. The closest RCMP station was in Vegreville, almost thirty miles away. There was nowhere to lock up a prisoner. Amhurst only had one decent hotel. I would find Jake and his minders at the Royal Edward, and I'd make sure my old friend never had to go back to prison.

I called Carol as I walked out the front door. I dialled her number from memory. It was burned into my brain, from all those bleak nights when I'd punch in her number and then hang up before it could ring.

Her mother answered, giving me a cheerful "Merry Christmas!"

"I need to talk to Carol. Is she there?"

The cheer vanished from her voice. "Is that you, Ben?"

"I need to talk to her, Mrs. Kozinski. It's important."

"I don't think that's a good idea."

"All right, then, give her a message for me, please?" She wouldn't want to, but Mrs. Kozinski was too old-fashioned and uptight not to pass a message along. "Tell her Christine is in trouble."

"What! What kind of trouble?"

"She's fallen in with a bad crowd," I said. "It's not something you can help her with. She needs to get out of Amhurst. Away from bad influences. Don't worry, Carol and I can help her. I just need to take care of something first."

I hung up before she could question me. For the first time in ten long years I had a goal beyond the next score. I had a purpose, a task worth doing. I had to shoot my best friend, and then I had to change my life.

It wouldn't be easy, afterward. I didn't know how normal people lived. I didn't know how to set the kind of example Christine needed. But Carol knew. She would show me, and together we would make it work. She would save Christine.

She would save me.

The snow was deep, the air sharp and cold. "Hang on, Jake," I said as I pulled the balaclava down over my face. "Ben's coming." I plunged through the snow, revelling at the way the sun glittered on all those tiny flakes. I shoved my hands into my pockets and felt the comforting weight of the pistol. "Hang on, Christine. Hang on, Carol. I'm coming." I wrapped my hand around the butt of the gun.

"I'm going to make everything all right."

# Of Gathering Gloom
## Jessica McHugh

The last maple bacon donut sold an hour ago, and *Christmas Shoes* has played four times straight. In the achy melancholy of Dresden Towne Mall, sugar-starved shoppers clog the Farmer Bakery, their patience thinned by the maddening pulse of the blue icicle lights festooning the walls. It outshines even the garish North Pole display in the middle of the mall, where I sit on a throne surrounded by fake trees, fake snow, and bulletproof glass.

When I first became the "holiday guy" at Dresden Towne Mall, it was a shining star of suburban commerce, but the recession hit Dresden hard, forcing the upper crust to close shop and find a community that didn't pride itself on clinging to the bowl when the economy hit flush. The second level has been closed off for nearly a year, the escalators now somber stairs leading to boarded stores and a food court closed so quickly that many believe the Long Wok fryer baskets are still submerged in stagnant grease. With holiday attendance in decline, management almost didn't hire me to play Santa this year, but after an attempted robbery of Farmer Bakery around Easter, they decided the town needed Santa Claus more than ever. Especially since I was the one who intercepted both the robber and his stray bullet. Hero status doesn't help business though. While the gourmet donut shop is busier than ever, I suffer poor patronage *and* a limp thanks to the bullet fragments still embedded in my right thigh. The barrier around the throne is overkill, and the tattered reindeer with the faded nose is a poor substitute for Santa's lap, but I don't fight the safety measure. It's not that I'm afraid of being shot again, and though Dresden's citizens are especially ravenous this week, it's not the shoppers I fear. It's their sneering and gagging I want to avoid, along with the raging nausea that rises from the crowd when my rancid body odor runs loose in public.

I can't pinpoint the stench's origin. My armpits are two of the nastiest culprits, I wager, but the stink's ranker than your run-of-the-mill BO. It's mustier, and it shifts at the drop of a hat from a sour mothball smell to something piercing and fecal. It could be my fake beard, I suppose. No matter how often I clean it, the matted white hair smells of sewage and corn chips. It's a miracle the people of Dresden have put up with me this long. The least I can do is stay behind the glass.

I count the minutes until my shift ends and I can leave this reeking bubble, but I won't be able to relax until Janet's shift ends too. Due to my sluggish recovery, I was forced to hire the plump and lovely Janet Smalls as a housekeeper and caretaker. She cleans and stocks the house while I'm at work, but she also drives me to and from the mall and helps me settle in at home. The quiet woman in her mid-thirties is the last person I want to inhale my putrid stench, but she's also the kindest about it. When I feel like a mosquito cloud of nauseants and launch into self-depreciation, Janet cuts through my shit, shakes her head, and says, "Just be yourself. Be happy." She pretends I'm

## IT'S A WEIRD WINTER WONDERLAND

a normal man, and I desperately wish I could treat her like a normal woman, to pull her close like I don't have myriad dumpster scents radiating from my crotch. It's a stupid dream. Even the dozen pine-scented air fresheners I wear under my Santa suit aren't strong enough to block my natural foulness. On certain days, the sweaty trees only make it worse.

That's how I feel now, pine and putridity amalgamating into a toxic gas that fills the bulletproof box. Two tubby runts with sticky faces stand in line at the North Pole, but they're not paying attention when I wave them forward. Instead, they stare at their mother in the line at the baker. The crowd grows thicker and bolder, and she's in serious threat of losing her place to the violent mosh pit.

I clear my throat and boom to the children. "Ho, Ho, Ho! Merry Christmas!"

The first kid swivels his head and squints. "Don't you mean *Happy Holidays*?" Behind him, the shorter boy folds his arms over his ample chest.

"Is that what you'd like from Santa? Political correctness?" My beard smells like dog paws, but it hides my smirk. "Hop up on Rudolph and tell Santa all about it."

The smirk melts the moment the kid obeys. Anxious sweat soaks my beard, and my velvety red suit becomes an oven. One would think baking human meat would smell better than this. By the time the kid mounts the reindeer, the glass cage reeks of crusty socks soaked in piss and blue cheese. It's unlikely my stench escapes the box, but the little boy glares like he's just seen a zombie orangutan vomiting in a patch of skunk cabbage.

"What's your name, little boy?"

"Franklin."

"And what do you want for the holidays, Franklin?"

"Donuts," he says with a resolute nod.

"That's all?"

"Well, I guess I wouldn't mind if my brother died."

My voice catches in my throat. "I'm sorry?"

"My brother," he says, gesturing to his roly-poly sibling. "I don't like him. He can drop dead any time."

The side door between The Slicery and All the Balls Sporting Goods swings open, and several people scream bloody murder. Franklin leaps off the deer and jumps up and down while shrieking, "They're here, they're here!"

## IT'S A WEIRD WINTER WONDERLAND

Merrill Farmer emerges, pushing an enormous cart stacked with donut boxes, and the crowd cheers like he's an elusive movie star. Hal figures the president of Farmer Bakery must be a wealthy man, but he doesn't act like it. He wears simple coveralls, moves like molasses, and disregards my greeting whenever he passes the North Pole.

As the brothers dash after the donut man pushing through the horde to his store, I sit frozen in sweaty shock from the boy's holiday wish. I couldn't have heard him right. I was so focused on whether he could smell me through the glass, I must have imagined the horrific response.

A wet slap against the enclosure steals my attention, and I groan at the mangy terrier smashing its nose against the glass.

"Dammit, Merrill! The dog!"

The donut guy is too deep in sugar-starved zealots to hear me. Even if I were sitting on Rudolph, I doubt Merrill would acknowledge my complaints about the stray terrier he keeps letting slip into the mall. It's the fourth time this week I've had to leave my safe space to usher out the mutt.

Upon exiting the enclosure, the sweet wafting warmth of Farmer Bakery immediately grabs me by the nose, but it's no match for the nasty pup propelling loud, smelly yaps.

Large patches of dirty fur are missing from its belly, and while some of the exposed skin is scabbed over, some sections weep yellow pus. There are knots of crusty hair on its legs that I hope is more mud than feces but ultimately decide not to ponder it too deep.

Holding my breath because of the dog's stink and keeping my arms glued to my sides because of mine, I limp and nudge the terrier to the employee exit. I urge it into the back hall. It barks and tries to dart back into the mall, but with a nimble spin I manage to close the door behind us. Agony shoots through my leg as I twist around, realizing a second too late I'm expelling malodorous frustration into the face of a fellow mall employee. I cover my mouth and apologize to the beautiful young woman, then bolt past her to the exit with the dog trailing dutifully behind.

"How was it today?"

## IT'S A WEIRD WINTER WONDERLAND

Janet Smalls looks in the rearview mirror every few seconds, and I do my best to avoid meeting her gaze.

"Slow."

"This close to Christmas?"

I adjust myself in the back seat. My leg aches terribly from the stunt with the dog—the bullet fragments feel like they've traveled down to my knee—but I don't want Janet to know. The more she worries, the longer she'll stay.

When she stops at the curb in front of the house, I insist that she head home, but she ignores me. Not the way Merrill does. My words bounce off Merrill's leathery skin like gnats, but Janet absorbs them. She may not obey every request, but she takes them on board like cataloging the distinct fragrances of wildflowers.

I don't know anything about Janet's personal life—just that she spends most of her day shuttling me around and tidying my home—but I recognize the loneliness in her eyes. Through every giggle and "Yes, of course, Mr. Parker," I see a soul in need.

It might be projection, but I'll never know; even when she helps me into the house and asks if I'm in pain, I'm locked up tight. Sitting me on the couch is like trying to fold a table lamp. I eventually fall to the sofa, wincing as she crouches to unlace my boots.

"The candles, Janet."

With a small exhalation, she nods. "Yes, of course, Mr. Parker."

The reindeer appliques on her sweater jangle when she hops up. If it were anyone else, I'd suspect the jingle bell noses would annoy me, especially after an unsuccessful day at the North Pole, but each little chime is a love hymn she doesn't know she's singing.

"Mr. Parker!"

"What? I didn't say anything."

"Is your leg okay? You're bleeding." She starts toward me, but I back away.

"The candles. Light the candles."

She sighs heavily and continues lighting the remaining ten of thirty-two candles adorning the surfaces of my home. Evergreen and gingerbread scents tumble with clean cotton and hydrangea, and notes of citrus breeze bring up the rear with a cinnamon smack. As I inhale in gratitude, I notice Janet exhaling in slow, shuddering breaths. The candles must not be enough to mask my stink. The poor woman must be in hell.

## IT'S A WEIRD WINTER WONDERLAND

She's excellent at hiding her disgust as she crouches again and says, "Will you let me have a look at your leg?"

I grit my teeth as I remove the first aid kit from the coffee table drawer. "I'll be fine. You can go."

"Nonsense. I know you hired me to clean, but I've taken plenty of first aid classes. I know what I'm doing. Please, I'm here to help you." She reaches for my belt, but I block her hand and sheepishly apologize.

"No, it's my fault," she says, standing. "You don't want my help, and I should respect that."

"It's not that I don't appreciate it."

"It's for the best. I'm on the edge of a migraine, to be honest. I'm already getting those floating orb things."

"Again? Have you seen a doctor?"

"Yes, and it's nothing serious. It's just the, um..." She glances around the room. "The candles, you know. All the different scents; it's a lot to take in."

She's so kind, so accommodating. It's sweet of her to pretend it's the candles and not my hotdog water odor that aggravates her. Even as she massages her forehead, she smiles and graciously accepts my apology. "It's your house," she says, "and you *are* paying me to be here."

My heart sinks. Janet is only here because of the money, only *kind* because of the money. I always knew it deep down, but I hoped never to have the proof. And as much as I don't wish her pain, I can't snuff the candles for fear of exposing my true stench. Even money wouldn't get her through the door after that.

She breathes through the pain and rubs her temples with both hands. "If it's okay, I think I should go. I'm not feeling so good."

"Of course you're not." Forcing a tight smile, I reach for my wallet, but Janet doubles over before she can take the cash.

She claps her hand over her mouth, but the upheaval can't be stopped. Her splayed fingers actually give the vomit a broader spray. It spatters the rooms and extinguishes several candles. Her hand drips, but she keeps it cupped over her mouth as she sobs apologies.

"Don't worry about it," I tell her. "These things happen. Just sit down and relax. I'll get a towel."

I limp to the closet, but Janet Smalls is gone before I reach it. When the front door slams, all that remains is what she's left on the table, the carpet, and dripping from the Christmas tree. I sit on the edge of the couch knowing I should clean

## IT'S A WEIRD WINTER WONDERLAND

up the mess, but inhaling the stench incites a sly smile. For once, it doesn't come from me.

???

Janet doesn't show up for work the next day. She doesn't call or show the day after either. When three days pass without a word, I figure I'll never see her again. I've feared this since I hired her, but after a few weeks I'd nearly convinced myself it was irrational. I'd even convinced myself Janet liked me as a person—or at least didn't mind interacting with me. It was a quiet voice that seldom broke through the haze of self-loathing, but when I was with Janet, the voice was loud and clear: "Be yourself, be happy."

Nothing about being myself makes me happy, especially not after stinking up a cab first thing in the morning. I give the donut-munching driver a large tip, but the money is too rank and greasy for the driver to touch.

He sucks sugary glaze from his fingers so hard that the nail on his pointer finger shifts slightly. Pink slime oozes from under the disturbed nail, but he licks it up as readily as donut cream.

I don't realize I'm staring until he says, "Drop it on my lap, asshole."

I sigh and release the sweaty bills over the cabbie's legs. Snorting, the man closes his sticky fingers on the steering wheel and peals away.

"Where's your wife?"

I pull up my beard and turn to the young woman from Perfume Palace. I've never noticed how her largest smile reveals an asymmetrical dimple that changes and brightens her face. It's almost cruel when she shifts out of the expression, like her dimple was the solitary star in a now jet-black sky.

"My wife?"

"The woman who usually drops you off."

*Janet*. It's the first time someone inferred we were married, but certainly not the first time I've imagined it. I never expected anything of her, but there were days when her kindness seemed a proposal—for companionship at the very least.

"She's not— "

"Oh, I'm sorry. I didn't mean to pry."

"She worked for me. I had trouble getting around after the incident."

"Of course, the shooting." She squeezes my arm, pulling herself close enough to lower my beard.

I hold my breath, which makes me sweat, and I pray for a skunk to miraculously appear, get angry, and spray us both.

"I never told you how brave I thought that was," she continues. "You didn't have to stand up to that robber."

"Anyone would've done the same."

"If that were true, someone would've beat you to it."

I shrug, and she tilts her head. "Does it hurt?"

"It's fine."

"You're a real hero, you know that?"

I fake a sneeze and pull away, apologizing and sniffling as I pull up my beard again. Despite the matted curls' contribution to my stench, I feel more secure behind the costume, like my face doesn't deserve the exposure. Perhaps it doesn't. I haven't done anything so well as hide it inside an icon.

A raspy yapping catches my attention, and I groan as the ratty terrier gallops toward me.

"Oh, it's your dog!" the young woman says.

"Not my dog, not my wife, definitely not my day," I grumble as I start toward the employee entrance.

"I don't want to bother you," she says, keeping up with my limping gait. "I just wanted to check that you're okay. I haven't gotten the chance to apologize since I ran into you the other day."

"It was my fault," I say, searching my pockets for my ID and nudging away the dog.

She pulls out her ID and swipes it in the door lock. The picture of Gloria Weaver, Assistant Manager and Aroma Specialist at the Perfume Palace is a smiley one, but her dimple is strikingly absent.

"It's a horrible picture, isn't it?"

I shake my head. "It just doesn't look like you."

Opening the door, she hums the chorus of *Christmas Shoes*, and closes the door before the dog can dart inside. "I bet yours doesn't look like you, either. Unless they made you take the picture with the Santa beard."

"No picture."

"That's not fair!" The woman skitters and gets ahead of me, dancing backward and rolling off the walls as we walk the back hall. She crinkles her brow and gnaws on her bottom lip.

I avert my face and exhale against my palm to check my breath. I could swear it stinks of pickles, but I haven't eaten a pickle in months. My armpits drip humiliation down my ribcage.

"Hey, you can talk to me, Hal."

## IT'S A WEIRD WINTER WONDERLAND

With a smile that displays her perfect white teeth, she says, "I'm Gloria."

I clear my throat. "Hal."

"Yes, I know," she says through a chuckle. "You know, I've worked here as long as you have, and I never see you talk to anyone. Kids and their parents, sure, but you don't seem to socialize much. I rarely see you outside your cage these days. Why is that?"

"I... I guess I have issues."

"Don't we all?" she says with a wink and opens the inner door.

I thank her sheepishly and make a beeline for my bulletproof sanctuary, pushing through a group of greasy teens who work at the Seems Like TV store. They grunt insults and snicker through patchy facial hair, but I've trained myself to ignore them. I'm not sure about Gloria, though.

I turn to defend her from the brats, but she cuts through their stunned crew like Moses through the Red Sea—if Moses and his blessed staff were a curvaceous woman and the promise of a one-dimpled smile.

She marches past them and up the stairs to the reindeer, which she straddles with a forceful laugh. I try not to look right at her, like the ease of her beauty might burn my retinas, but desire betrays me. I keep slipping back to her smooth tan skin, her crooked mouth, her chest rising and falling with a calm I've never known.

Especially not now. My rapid breath threatens to propel my heart from my chest and end my useless life. God, how horrible would a death like that smell?

Imagination is a summoning spell. Every breath is a rotten corpse now, which I swallow hard while praying they don't slip out the other end. I quickly shut myself inside the glass enclosure.

She drums the box with manicured fingernails, and her focus slides up to mine as she says, "I was thinking we could grab a drink tonight."

"Sorry, I can't." I answer without an excuse, and when Gloria offers me one, I fall right into her trap.

"Is it your leg?"

"Yes."

"But you said you were fine. Were you lying to me?"

The beard is soggy and smells of spoiled yogurt. I'm certain it leaves a smear of milky run-off when I pull it down around my neck. "I wouldn't do that."

# IT'S A WEIRD WINTER WONDERLAND

The statement appears to amuse and vindicate her. "So, you're free tonight."

"Yes, I'm free," I reply through a groaning sigh.

"Don't sound so excited, Hally." She dismounts Rudolph with a giggle. "Drinks after close? Maybe supper? I'll meet you here...at the deer."

When I nod, she bites her bottom lip and curls her mouth—not enough for the dimple, but close enough to convince me if only for a moment that I'm not the most repulsive creature on Earth.

"Oh, I nearly forgot." She pulls a small box from her pocket and sets it atop Rudolph's snout. "For you."

"What is it?"

"A present."

"From who?"

"From me, silly."

She leans to the window, and her breath flowers on the glass. Dragging her fingers, she cuts a heart into the fog.

My neck twitches under the duress of my rapid pulse. Sweat drips down my throat, over my chest, and collects at my waistband. I flap my velvety top to get some airflow and stares at it like it might explode in my hand. "Why would you give me a present?"

"I get the feeling it's been a while since someone gave you one. Besides, I'm a people-pleaser. Call it a stupid obsession, but I eat that stuff up."

"I don't think it's stupid."

"Good. You can wear it tonight."

As she struts down the stairs, I for once don't care about whatever stench I emit. I slip out of the enclosure and snatch her gift. Palming the box, I lift the lid with a smile that's promptly destroyed by the tiny bottle of cologne in a cotton nest.

Gloria's voice repeats in my mind, *"Wear it tonight,"* and adds viciously, *"I won't be able to stand your stench without it."*

My eyes well with tears when I exhale.

One of the teenage boys nearby howls loudly and covers his nose. "*Jesusfuck*, Craig, did you just rip one? It smells like rotten fish. You need to clean out your asshole, son."

"It wasn't me, I swear," Craig says, his voice reaching a soprano pitch. In a red-faced panic, he points at Hal. "It was that Santa dude. The other day, he ripped a fart so rank it cracked the glass. The mall stunk for hours. Don't you remember?"

## IT'S A WEIRD WINTER WONDERLAND

"Is that what it was?" another boy squeals. "Shit, I thought a kid had puked or something. I didn't know it was Santa's ass!"

I clench my jaw as everyone in earshot stares, Gloria included. She looks embarrassed to have been seen with me, but she doesn't say anything. She doesn't indicate she'll be canceling our plans, and she doesn't need to. She's wised up, like the rest. Why waste the energy it would take to cancel?

The day moves so slow I almost forget to take a lunch break, but a nagging voice in my head, along with hunger pains, eventually coaxes me from my glass shell. It's the same voice that tells me the elderly mall walkers are wincing at me instead of their aching joints, that the teens infesting my periphery think I'm as insignificant as the dried-up fountains they carve with obscenities. It's the voice that walks empty paths and insists they were teeming with people before I limped along. I walk slower, and it speaks louder. It tells me I've should've brushed my tongue one more time, added just one more swipe of deodorant, stuffed my underwear with dryer sheets. Until then, I'm walking garbage, and everyone in Dresden knows it.

But Gloria Weaver acted doubtful, so when the voice seizes my mobility in the vicinity of Perfume Palace, I can't help feeling a twinge of serendipity. It's followed by an eggy heat that leaks from my costume and clashes with the aroma wafting from the nearby pretzel cart. Using the cart as camouflage, I stare at the only store in a line of four with the lights still on—most of them, anyway. One of the A's in "Palace" has burned out, reducing royalty to commoner. But there's nothing common about Gloria. Even leaning on the counter, supporting her face on her fist while reading an ebook, she's the most regal sight in Dresden Mall. When a customer waddles in, Gloria dutifully sets down her Kindle and smiles. It's genuine enough to fool the customer, but it's too tight and creaseless to be real.

The pretzel salesperson leans around her cart, her face beaming hope. "What can I get you, Mr. Claus? Or is it Mr. Kringle?"

"Oh, no, I'm just– "

The woman's eyes soften with disappointment, and I adjust the prop glasses balanced on my nose.

"It's Hal," I say, "and I'll have a sea salt and rosemary pretzel, please."

## IT'S A WEIRD WINTER WONDERLAND

The woman looks like she might leap into the air with whooping joy, but she confines her excitement to her tiptoes. She cavorts as she plucks a pretzel from the rack, drops it in a bag, and hands it over.

"That'll be seven dollars, please."

I nearly drop the bag. "Seven dollars for one pretzel?"

"I'm afraid so," she says after a dejected sigh. "I had to raise my prices after Farmer's came out with their maple bacon donuts."

As I fish out my wallet, I notice a thin stream of blood rolling from her nose.

"Miss, there's uh..." I point and she presses her hand to her nose.

Looking at her bloody fingers, she scowls. "Rather rude of you, don't you think?"

"I'm sorry?"

"Maybe I like being free and easy like this. But no, you men have to get all up in our bloody bits, don't you? Can't mind your own damn business." She extends her clean hand. "Seven dollars."

I stutter, clutching the bag to my chest. "I'm sorry. I didn't mean to upset you."

"Yes, because we women are so emotional. It's no wonder people don't believe in you anymore." Her face cracks into a smile, and she chuckles heartily. "Would you mind tottling off and getting me a donut, dearie?"

"I should probably be getting back to the North Pole."

"Yes, yes, good idea. I shouldn't eat another today anyway. I still think it's a bit unfair how Farmer swooped in and stole all the business. It stinks to high heaven."

I shrink back. "Stinks?"

"Sure. It's fishy, don't you think?"

My stench, like corroded copper in an amusement park bathroom, overwhelms the pretzels now. As I stumble away, arms pinned to my sides and mouth clamped shut, I lob my gaze to Gloria Weaver one last time. She sprays an atomizer at a customer, prompting the lady to sneeze. Distracted, I don't see the little boy headed my way, and I walk straight into him, knocking both the boy and his half-eaten donut to the floor.

The child whines until the donut is in his mouth again, like a baby with a teething ring, but satisfaction soon turns ferocious. His sugar-glazed lips tighten as they draw back from his teeth in a snarl. His teeth part, and he opens his mouth wide to take the remainder of the donut in one violent stuff. The pastry puffs up his cheeks as he munches, and after a strained gulp, he narrows his eyes, puckers his lips, and spits.

A bloody tooth hits me in the belly and bounces to the floor. He fires another, sticking in my beard, and one more that leaves a string of spittle on my pants.

I backpedal in revulsion and trip over my feet, and my tailbone hits the floor with a smack that shoots pain up and down my spine. When my scream draws the attention of those nearby, the boy collects his teeth and flashes a bloody grin before dashing away. The pretzel lady and a few others rush to help, but I scramble to my feet and retreat to the wall. Looking back to Perfume Palace, I find Gloria's gaze without effort. She stands agog, head tilted, and rigidly waves at me. Drenched in reeking terror, I sprint for the nearest exit.

The mangy dog is waiting when I burst from the side door. While customers veer away from the panting Santa who slumps to the ground, the foul-smelling creature jogs up with its black-spotted tongue hanging out the side of its mouth.

I rub my eyes like it'll erase the horror. "What the hell's going on? What's wrong with me?"

As if answering, the dog plants its butt on my boot. With a phlegmy bark, it scratches a scabby patch behind its ear, prompting a line of fleas to skitter down its cheek.

I shudder but take comfort that I'm not as bad off as the dog. It reeks so terribly I might be considered fragrant in comparison. Staring into the creature's watery eyes, its odor barrels up my nostrils when it barks.

I grin. "You're a good girl, aren't you?"

She pants joyfully, and I scratch the cleanest part of the dog's head with one finger. I've never had a pet before, but it seems as good a time as any to adopt.

The Dollar Diver has candy cane-striped collars and leashes that look like they might fall apart in the rain, but they'll do in a pinch. The stray is astonishingly calm when I buckle the collar, and although the combination of our respective smells brings tears to my eyes, I'm eager to blame them all on the dog. In the few minutes the pup and I spend in the bathroom, we turn the bleach-scented refuge with hints of rancid wind into a full-blown shitstorm. I change out of my Santa outfit and douse myself in Gloria's cologne—under my arms, through my hair, and in every crotch crevice—before I'm acceptable enough for the date.

"If she even shows up," I say to the mirror, but it's not the mirror that responds, "She will."

The feminine voice echoes in the bathroom, and I duck beneath the stalls to check for feet.

I'm alone. The dog follows me on the quest to prove I didn't imagine it, trying to lick my face every time I stoop down. I finally let her reeking tongue touch my cheek, then wipe the saliva away and apply the rest of the cologne. The strong aroma makes my head spin, and I brace myself on the sink as the pup makes a gagging noise. I jump back, afraid it's going to yak on my shoes, but the mutt swallows its vomit and flashes a canine grin.

"I guess I might as well get it over with, eh?"

"Yup." The dog flops out her tongue and pants with gleeful, gangrenous breaths as I squint into her watery eyes. She tries to lick me again, but I dodge her tongue and snatch up the leash.

When I open the door, the terrier gallops out first, leaving a fresh cloud of swamp gas for me to limp through.

Gloria's leaning on Rudolph when I exit the back hall, and my sweat glands kick into high gear. Cologne drips down my forehead and stings my eyes. I wipe it away with my sleeve and blink through the pain as I shuffle to the North Pole. I must look like some near-sighted Igor hosting a hurricane in my skin, but Gloria's expression doesn't twist in revulsion as I near.

Her attitude is a wink at a funeral. The mall is gloomy at closing time, but Gloria's dimple brings out the sun as she strides forward. "I knew it would smell good on you," she says. Dressed in a slinky black number adored with delicate silver chains that waterfall down her neck, she stands with one hip popped and both lips in a dangerous pucker. Her hair is twisted up in a style only women know the name for, but I imagine she invented it just for tonight.

"I'm glad you showed," she says. "After what happened earlier– "

"Nothing happened."

Her eyebrows knit in sympathy. "Yes, of course."

The dog barks, and Gloria's focus icily shifts downward.

"Are you bringing the stray along?"

I clench my teeth and nod. "She's not a stray anymore. She's mine."

## IT'S A WEIRD WINTER WONDERLAND

"Oh. What's her name?" Gloria pats the dog's head and coughs as a cloud of dirt billows from the fur. Pulling wet wipes from her purse, she cleans her hands with a snarl.

"Her name's Dusty," I reply quickly.

The dog's spotted tongue flops out, and she tilts her head at Gloria. Following a prolonged squeak, the smell of rotten eggs rises from Dusty's scabby butt.

Gloria covers her nose, and I apologize. "I know I shouldn't have brought her along, but she's getting on in years. Now that I've found her, I don't want to leave her alone just in case...you know..."

She lowers her hand, but it's clear she's doing her damnedest to breathe through her mouth. Squeezing my shoulder, she bats her eyelashes. "I understand. It's sweet."

"Speaking of which, you look..." I wring the leash in my sweaty hands. "I didn't know I was supposed to get fancy."

"Oh," she says, sliding one leg out the slit in her dress. "Is this fancy?"

Dusty barks, and she snaps her leg back in.

"Where do you want to go?" I ask, drumming my chin. "I think there's an Outback in walking distance. Or maybe that closed."

She shakes her head, then rolls her focus to the second level of Dresden Towne Mall. "I was thinking of somewhere a little closer." Tugging on my shirt, she chuckles. "Didn't you know the top floor opens up after close?"

"It does?"

"Oh...a virgin," she hums. Her tongue flicks her top teeth and she curls her finger at me. "Follow me. And don't worry, I'll be gentle."

Gloria's hips swish like the pendulum of an antique clock—a priceless hypnosis that leads me up the broken escalator. I don't mean to stare, but it's fascinating how the lower half of her body moves like she has gliding and pivoting joints where I have fixed bone.

Dusty tugs the leash until I'm shoulder to shoulder with Gloria on the escalator. She links her arm with mine, and we stride in surprisingly effortless rhythm up the remaining steps while the level one lights click off. Beads of sour sweat burst from my pores. Even with Dusty there, I'm convinced Gloria will smell past the cologne and canine grime to my malodorous garbage scent. Every time her nose crinkles, I try to pull away, but she doesn't allow it.

## IT'S A WEIRD WINTER WONDERLAND

The second floor is quiet except for the sound of torn posters flapping on empty display cases—the whispers of middle class ghosts who think real stores like Sears and The Gap will return any day now. In the cobwebbed dark, I'm surprised to find many of the second-floor rumors true. Mannequins stand in compromising positions in and outside of shops, and a family of raccoons is living in the high-end electronics store. But as we approach the once bustling food court, specks of light blink on ahead. Jury-rigged lamps illuminate a path leading to the dining area, which wears a festive wardrobe outclassing any in Dresden Towne Mall—until a chain of icicles bathe the food court in abrasive blue light.

When Merrill Farmer waddles out of Long Wok, I stop in my tracks. He and other mall employees emerge from abandoned kitchens and counters, congregating by a steaming ten-gallon tank where an ornate carousel once sat. Time has taken its toll on the floors and walls. Rotted holes surround us like booby traps that the other employees treat like harmless rain puddles.

"Come in, come in," Merrill says in a voice that sounds too loud for his small frame. "And who do we have here?"

Gloria tows me, I tow Dusty, and Dusty blows out a fart smelling of old crabmeat and motor oil. A portly gentleman from the gag gift shop, "Boners," marches out from a cookie pizza place and trumpets Gloria's name. He flings his arms around her, and they exchange air kisses before the man squints at me over the rim of his glasses.

"No outsiders, Glori. That's the rule."

She cuddles up to me with a high-pitched giggle. "Oh, you kidders. You know Hal!" Met with blank stares, she adds, "Santa Claus."

"Oh, the Easter Bunny," Stanley says, but a teenager from the Seems Like TV store wheezes in amusement.

"Nah, son, that's the Tom turkey dude. And the fuckin' jack-o-lantern that hands out candy on Halloween."

"All and more," I say. "Good evening." I speak in shallow breaths to limit the amount of stink I emit, but I have to be careful not to hold back too much. I've practiced, but I still get lightheaded if I go overboard.

Dusty scratches behind her ear, and a wet scab falls to the floor. Several employees back away. A skeletal woman from Jort Fashions claps her hand to her mouth like she's going to throw up.

## IT'S A WEIRD WINTER WONDERLAND

"I know I didn't let the mutt in this time," Merrill snarls as Dusty sniffs his shoe.

I gently tug the dog back. "Sorry about that. I decided to adopt her."

Stanley's lips twist and shrivel like they're trying to escape down his throat. "Glori, sweetheart, you know I'd do anything for you, but this is too much. The smell is unbearable."

As I shrink back in humiliation, Gloria digs a tampon out of her purse and tosses it at him. "Cut it in half and become a mouth breather, darling, because the dog's here to stay."

Stanley catches and throws the tampon like it's an active grenade, and Gloria's metronome ass beats him back as she leads me to a table orbed in neon light.

Dizziness washes over me. I quickly slump into the seat, inhaling and exhaling deep breaths at the floor. Dusty yips, and I shush her, wrapping her leash around the leg of my chair. The dog sighs, and a rancid odor rises. Gloria laughs as she waves away the smell, but the others aren't so amused. They stand between the dog and the steaming vat like dutiful soldiers.

Shaking off the faintness, I point to the tank. "What is that thing?"

"Salvation," Merrill answers. He's been a quiet troll of a man in the past, but he's a boss up here. He rounds the vat like its contents are holy gold and my presence has depreciated the value.

"It's filling for the maple bacon donuts," Gloria says. "He thought it would be safer making it up here after the attempted robbery. Speaking of which…" She spins on her chair and sneers at the donut guy. "…you owe Hal a thank you, don't you think?"

"You don't owe me anything," I say. The bullet fragments are aflame inside me, and I massage the wound as I take a deep, downturned breath. "I don't want to talk about that. I just want to take it easy tonight."

Gloria leans across the table and lays her silky hand upon my shit-drenched mitt.

"That's fine. Let's talk about something else. What do you do when you're not behind bulletproof glass, Hal?"

I don't know how to respond because my personal interests don't extend beyond finding new ways to overpower my odor.

"Not much. I have…" My brain feels as cobwebbed as the corners of the abandoned Foot

Locker as I search for the right word. "Issues, I have issues."

She touches my hand, and her dimple greets me like a holy disciple. "Those things don't matter to me."

"You don't know what they are."

"So, tell me. Let me decide for myself."

When I exhale, my vision blurs and crosses. A sudden nausea rises from my gut, and I groan through mounting dizziness. The room spins, and I grip the tablecloth. "Gloria, I don't feel so well."

She hums as she reclines in her chair and taps the armrest. "No, I suspected you wouldn't. But I didn't think it would make you this ill. It's just supposed to knock you out."

"What do you mean?"

"The cologne. You must've used a lot to combat your..." She giggles. "...issues."

Dusty is barking like mad, but I can't quiet her; I can barely hold up my head. When I crumple onto the table, the other Dresden Towne employees approach like starving lions stalking a wounded warthog. The teen growls and grabs for Dusty's collar.

The dog snaps at his hand and shifts the chair, knocking me to the floor, mumbling and drooling. Dusty uses the opportunity to unwrap her leash, and though a man from Moore Guns lunges at her, she bolts from food court and into the gloom.

"Leave the mutt," Merrill says. "How much you give him anyway? He looks purple."

"I didn't expect him to use it all. It doesn't matter anyway, as long as his second comes out of hiding, we don't need the watchman conscious."

My vision spirals and dims as Gloria crouches beside me.

"Don't be afraid," she says. "We're here to help."

I awaken to Gloria's dimpled smile and weeping gratitude. "You're awake, thank goodness."

"What happened to me?"

Gloria reaches out, her fingers curled to caress my cheek, but an icy aura surrounds her hand and I jerk away. She pulls back and sits up straight in her chair. "We're not the enemies here, darling."

"Why would I have any enemies? I haven't done anything wrong."

"It's not what you've done. It's what you *are*," she says. "At least, what you *were* before they did this to you. This...curse."

## IT'S A WEIRD WINTER WONDERLAND

I'm not mindful of my breath when I ask her what she means, and a stench like rotten milk and ammonia leaks from my taste buds. My head droops, and Gloria breathes through her mouth as she sidles up next to me.

"There's been a change of plans. We were trying to lure whoever did this to you out of hiding, but it's not working. Until then, we can't save Dresden."

"This is insane. It's—" My stomach churns, and a penny stench rises from my throat. "It's a disease, isn't it? A tumor or an infection. A blood clot from the bullet. These hallucinations, that kid spitting out his teeth—they're symptoms of something much worse."

"You have no idea," Stanley says.

"And that's the problem," Gloria adds. "Whoever cursed you stole your memory. It's real what you've been seeing from the people of Dresden. Your enemies have chosen wisely. When a town crumbles like this one, they swoop in and lay claim to the citizens."

She's talking nonsense, but this is more than anyone's said to me for months, except for kids and their impossible wishes. Merrill strides to the vat of donut cream, his nose in the air and hands clasped at his chest like he's about to launch into an operatic telling of Dresden's history. But he doesn't get a full word out before the teen gulps a large chunk of donut and says, "The place's infested with demons, Santa."

Stanley grabs the kid by the collar and drags him out of the dining area, back behind the counter of the Long Wok.

I'm the only one who laughs. Gloria and Merrill's faces are blank, their eyes averted.

"You *are* joking, right?"

Gloria exhales heavily. "I'm afraid not. It's a crude description, but the kid's technically right. These creatures are demonic entities. They possess and feast on human souls, especially those already weakened by the gathering gloom. You've felt it too, haven't you? You're drowning in it."

"What does any of this have to do with me?"

Leaning close, she unfolds her hand like a flower blossoming against my cheek. Her mouth is downturned, her eyes large and quivering. She's afraid, and it's no mystery why. Foulness rises from my skin like a ghost from a grave and she has to breathe through her mouth. Her voice is strained and hollow when she says, "You're the only one who can stop them."

## IT'S A WEIRD WINTER WONDERLAND

"I'm sorry, what?" I pull away, covering my mouth with my hand so I can breathe deeply. "Why do you think *I* can stop them? I'm a nobody. I'm just the guy who plays Santa."

"But you didn't used to be. Think back, far back. Years, decades. Where are you?"

It hurts to remember—like a butter knife poking my forehead from the inside—and I don't even get as far back as a decade. I can barely remember as far as a year, and there's nothing more than there's always been. The holidays, the mall, and the malodorous cologne rising from my bones.

I shake my head and it pounds. "Why can't I remember?"

"Because the demons got to you. They've gotten to everyone else in town too, but you're different. You're not one of them, Hal. You're their guardian."

I scoff. "Some shitty job I've done then."

"It's not your fault. These creatures are crafty, and they're extremely patient. But you are older, stronger. You are a celestial watchman, chosen to stand guard against these demons. Everything about you is built to sense these creatures. From dimensions away, you can smell their corruption and havoc. Unless..." She bops me on the nose. "Unless they muck up your sense of smell."

I chuckle at the absurdity, which summons an acidic cloud of bile and beef. I clap my hand to my mouth again, but Gloria eases it away.

"It's not real," she says. "They're messing with your head, Hally. That's why we were sent here. We worked ourselves into the Dresden community while we looked for ways to break your curse, but we haven't gotten very lucky. Now it's nearly too late. The citizens are already turning. Some to demons, some to food."

"The kid?"

She nods. "They don't even care that it's happening. Once they get a taste of the rot, they practically beg the demons to play footsie with their souls. Such simple creatures, these humans. When someone promises them a world without responsibility or consequence, it intoxicates them. The temptations wind them up and break them down and slowly reduce them to mush. Sometimes it takes days, sometimes years, and sometimes their victims become something else, something worse."

I don't know how I'm supposed to believe any of this, except for the fact that after all this time living in a rancid fog, thinking that it could be some supernatural mumbo jumbo gives me a sort of relief I haven't felt in... well, I can't say how long, can I? And if this is on the level, if I can be something more than the sour load I've become, I want it. I want to be the kind of man or guardian who matters, who people can depend on.

I stand up, chin lifted, and try my best to ignore the building fish oil stink. "What do I have to do?"

Gloria glances over her shoulder, and Merrill shuffles toward us holding a pink box filled with sticky donuts. The sugary scent pummels me when he opens the lid, and the donuts glisten like morning dew.

"You've never had one of these, have you?" he asks.

I shake my head. "I don't have much of a sweet tooth."

"Ah, but these are no ordinary sweets. These are special. Sacred, even."

I look to Gloria, whose face has tightened in watching the exchange. "What does this have to do with the curse?"

"Just trust us. Everything will seem better after you've eaten."

The sugary smell is cloying now, thick and snaking into my nostrils as Merrill pushes the donut closer and closer. The icicle lights sting my eyes, and the agony travels into my brain. I grit my teeth and turn away, but Gloria grabs me by the hair.

"Open your mouth."

I grunt in refusal, and Merrill pinches my nose to unclench my jaw.

"Open up," she screeches. "Open up, watchman!"

Just as my teeth part, Dusty leaps out from the shadows and closes hers on Gloria's ankle. She screams and kicks Dusty away, but the dog takes a chunk of her along. The teenager runs out from the back and leaps on top of Dusty, but the dog sinks her fangs into the kid's throat. Growling, she rips his neck to ribbons, exposing a whistling windpipe that calls more employees from recesses of the abandoned food court.

"What the hell is going on?"

Dusty tugs on my pants and runs, but I'm frozen to my spot. The employees howl, "Eat, watchman, eat" as they shamble closer, their focus burning so intently they don't notice Dusty tilting the donut cream tank until it's too late.

Gloria screams and Merrill falls to his knees in agonizing sorrow as the vat oozes and leaks into the holey floor. Stanley runs out, his hands to his face as he screams and tears into his flesh. It peels too easily, like warm putty submitting to his nails. With his skull dripping its own cream, he pulls a gun.

Dusty barks, and I break into a limping sprint. Dodging the sludge, the dog and I run into the cobwebbed dark, and the bullet follows.

I'm on the floor after the gunshot. I'm not hit, but my leg aches in sympathy as I search for Dusty. I find her several meters away, whining and panting in a small pool of blood, but the panic in her eyes softens when I bend over her. The bullet only grazed her leg, but it left fragments behind— bizarre, wriggling things that try to burrow into the wound. I pinch one of the spidery shards and toss it aside while approaching footsteps vibrate the crumbling floor.

Gazing deep into my eyes, the ratty terrier sounds like she howls, "Go."

Stanley and Merrill are in pursuit, and writhing shadows ride their heels. They call my name and tell me I'm a hero. They ask for applause, and the darkness obliges, roaring for me to come back, to receive my reward.

Dusty whines and paws my arm like she knows I'm considering it. I pat her cheek, and again she howls, "Go."

I stumble my way down to the first floor, where the world is bathed in the excruciating blue glow and slinging the torturous Christmas playlist from wall to wall. The exits are chained off and barricaded, and there's a furious bustling coming from the other end of the mall. I limp past the North Pole and the saggy ceiling above it, down the hallway, past the bathrooms, and to the seasonal storage room. Shivering in pain and terror, I tuck myself into a ball behind my massive Easter Bunny costume.

My leg aches worse than it did the day of the robbery, like the shrapnel's dividing, hollowing me out with slow revolutions that shred my muscle. Blood soaks through my pants, and my thigh feels like a swollen pimple that'll drive me mad if I don't pop it. Reaching into a nearby Easter basket, I smash a ceramic egg on the concrete and use a shard to slice into my pants. I expose the angry wound that's busted its bandages and leaks foul-smelling porridge. It's visibly throbbing—and squirming. There's something inside of me, and it's digging itself deeper. Tugging the rabbit mask closer, I bite down on a large pink ear. Then I dig deep too.

The wound's smell is dizzying *before* I plunge my fingers inside, but when the scab cracks and spills like a plum leaking hot milk, the stench of pork and Band-Aids consumes the oxygen. I wave the haze away and gulp for air as I hit something hard and slippery in my wound. Like the fragment in Dusty, it tries to wriggle away, but I hook my finger into its strange skin and drag it out. The spidery shard clings and claws to stay warm until, with a sloppy pop, I rip it out of my flesh. One by one, I remove the squirming metallic bits and throw them to the floor, crushing them under my boot. The pieces snap and die on the concrete, along with the reeking cloud that's been clogging up my brain since Easter.

My memory clears, and I feel weightless again. Being human is like wearing a ten-pound pendant on your chest at all times. It bashes your breast and crushes your heart until you can feel nothing but the heaviness of your humanity. But with my memory comes freedom. The pendant's weight is gone, and the feeling in my wings returns.

A collection of Christmas trimmings cut from the display in recent years sits nearby. The nativity, for one, and a cheap replica of The Grinch. And then there are the angels. I stare into their faded eyes, and for the first time in nearly a year, I stand without pain, without shame, and with the fortifying holiness of truth.

The door opens, and a voice croaks, "You're in here, aren't you?"

I duck as Merrill's hunched body blocks the hallway light, casting a deformed shadow over the plush costumes and props. I can smell his soul now, like microwaved feces and moldy pizza, and I know what he is.

"Why are you hiding?" the demon asks. "You led us to the one we've been hunting. We have the smelly little bitch that cursed you. She's been watching you for a long time. In the mall, in the parking lot, even in your own home." He snickers as he weaves through the stacks of holiday scenery, his voice clotted with deception. "It's funny when you think about it. You get hurt, and then you hire the same devil that's been poisoning you. And if that's not crazy enough, you adopt your tormenter while she's masquerading as a nasty mutt."

## IT'S A WEIRD WINTER WONDERLAND

My breath catches in my throat. *Janet*. She was sent here to help me. She's my real ally, and now they've got her. God, how stupid can I be?

I stand slowly, and Merrill's desperate gaze finds me in the costume gloom. He doesn't recognize that I've left Hal Parker in pieces beside an oversized Easter basket, so I play along.

"Is it true? Janet and Dusty are the same person?"

He nods. "Don't feel bad for not seeing it. It took us a while too, and *we're* not cursed. It can happen to any celestial—and it has a lot recently."

"What do you mean?"

Merrill rolls his shoulders. "There's a war on, Hal, and the enemy is winning. They are rebuilding this world as a factory farm for comrades and cattle."

I stutter a step and fake the pain, ducking to an overturned angel with a crooked halo.

"Come with me, Hal. We'll squash the little demon together. We'll make sure none of her friends can ever find her."

I wrench the halo from the angel's head as Merrill nears. Spotting the bullet fragments on the floor, he looses an ear-splitting screech and lunges at me. I swing the halo in a wide arc and slash his face in two. Cutting upwards, I liberate the donut guy's flesh like it's no more consistent than warm butter.

Hematite-colored sludge oozes down his shirt as he slides his fingertips into the widening wound. His skin flaps like a rubber mask as he stumbles backward and slips it off as effortlessly as a knit hat. Tossing his human face aside, Merrill hisses from the yolky black hollow in his smashed panoramic eggshell of a skull. I'd forgotten how ugly these bastards are. They have no noses, no ears, and no mouths unless you count the massive wet cavern below their slitted eyes.

Even without lips Merrill's voice is exactly the same when he hisses, "You old fool. You were better off in the curse. You would've had a pleasant death, like the humans you failed, and now it's going to hurt like hell."

I swipe at him again, slashing his throat and chest. I smash the halo into his cavernous face, and it shatters on his skull, but my fist continues on into the ebony slop. I don't quite punch out the back of his skull, but cold air seeps in through the cracks, tickling my knuckles while Merrill's mush contracts and twists around my wrist. I rip out my fist, and he falls to the floor with a splattering *whack*. As his guts run silvery black over the concrete, he continues to twitch and wheeze. "Wasn't lying," he says. "It's too late. Our children are in their veins."

Glaring down at the slime stain of a demon, I growl. "I'm a celestial watchman. It's never too late for me to save the world."

The employees of Dresden Towne Mall have gathered at the North Pole to feast. Some are on the menu, their bodies split open and spilling hematite jelly, while others engage in hedonistic activities that personify some of my nastiest former stenches. The ceiling sags from the overturned vat of hot donut cream, shadowing the snow-covered stage from the ghoulish blue light.

Beyond the Christmas music pumping from the speakers, there's a whimper and a jangle, and my focus flies to a woman collapsed on the stage, wearing a candy cane leash. Janet Smalls is scratched and gouged, but she's alive. A group of ravenous teens start toward her, blinded by power and death, and she forces herself to stand. As they storm the stage, she snatches one of the prop candy canes and swings it at the savages. She fights them off the stage, drops the candy cane, and locks herself in the bulletproof box.

I run up the stairs and stand beside the cage, scanning the crowd of newborn demons and living meals. "This ends now," I declare. "I know who I am, and I know what you've done, and I won't allow you to corrupt one more citizen of this town. This war is over."

Stanley is in the flickering blue, his face off-center and chewed up as he snacks on the pretzel lady's neck flab. "War?" he says, oiling forward. "Oh watchman, you don't know how right you are. The war has been over for months now—longer in the depths."

Those who haven't slipped their skin are well on their way. Their ears slide down the sides of their faces, and though a few are still losing teeth, most of their mouths are smooth caves of spit and gore.

"Don't you get it? This isn't the beginning, Hal. Dresden is one of the last to go."

Stanley drops his snack and rushes the stage. He tackles and wrestles me to the floor, but just as he's about to punch my lights out, Janet smacks the glass. He glances up at her, long enough for me to plunge my fingers into his face. He grunts and tries to pull free, but I'm hooked onto his innards, and the more he struggles the more he rips himself apart. Snatching a plastic peppermint shard with my other hand, I stab him in the throat, again and again, and a fountain of silver-black mud spouts from his deflating body. I roll away and his face collapses inward, melting from his crushed egg skull.

"Now, now, there's no cause for that." From behind the counter of Farmer Bakery, Gloria slides out with a trash bag swinging back and forth. On the edge of the blue light, she opens the bag and pours out dozens of donuts that whip the employees into a frenzy.

I inhale deeply and shudder. I recognize her now. Drenched in the reeking piss of rivalry, Gloria's stench assaults me with memories of our brutal encounters, of our various cons and threats since the beginning of mortal time. Corruption and death have foul and dizzying odors indeed, but no earthly scent compares to the one this ancient demon emits. On first whiff, she smells of tequila shits and molasses-glazed sardines, but there's a sinister layer of burnt hair that blooms last, like a bath bead that takes time to dissolve in the sinuses. The nearer she is, the harder it is too look at her for the cloying fumes radiating off her body; they burn and fill my eyes with tears. But in the bleariness, she's beautiful as ever, her gait still a charmer and voice alluring.

"My dear watchman," she says, "please don't cry. You failed, yes, but it was inevitable. You were outmatched. You can kill every creature here, but it won't do any good. You're too late. I'm not just in the blossoms of the world. I'm in the roots. I *am* the roots."

My wings twitch below my costume, aching more with her proximity. "You're lying," I say, and she giggles.

"No, I don't have to do that anymore. And you don't have to fight anymore," she says, smirking. "When the end comes—and it's coming soon—when the last human is turned and devoured, you don't have to remember that you could've saved them. You can be one of them again. A sad, smelly creature with nothing to live for. You were a wretch, for sure, but at least you didn't have a broken world on your shoulders."

It's the truth that never stops hurting, the war that never lets me rest, and she knows it. With as much celestial light that fills my soul, there is a spot of darkness that longs for sleep. I have faint memories of the days before the earth, when there were no wars to wage, no fools to protect, when I was my own man. And she was mine...

I look to Janet, and she's crying. She's crying for the same memories that fills me with inexorable sorrow.

"Oh Janet," I say, trembling. "I'm so sorry."

"No," she says, a small smile lifting her cheeks. "Don't be sorry, Mr. Parker. Be happy. Be yourself."

She presses her hand to the glass, and everything about her begs for me to meet her there, but the surrendering ceiling prevents me. Screeches and snaps resound through Dresden Towne Mall, and I jump back before a shower of scalding slop pours down from the second floor. The bulletproof box is surprisingly ineffective against the donut cream. It softens the glass, warping the door and trapping Janet as the tank slips and shudders through the soggy floor.

The impact blasts me off the stage, and I crack my head on the tile. My brain flashes with color and noise, and all the loathsome odors that masked the truth become nothing compared to the stench churning off Janet's crushed and molten corpse.

"What a waste," Gloria says. "All those babies will never know the joy of consumption. We've plenty of embryos to spare, but still, it's a bloody shame."

Gloria's fog is all around me now. Her lips touch my neck, and her hot fingers close around my biceps. She turns me away from the sickening scene and toward her dimpled smile.

"You look tired, darling. And hungry."

Plucking a donut from the floor, she holds it to my mouth. "One bite, and this can all be a dream. No more fighting, no failure, no death."

"You can't do that."

"Ah, but I can. The tables have turned, and power's gone with it. God didn't consult your kind when He made mortals or when He decided your people had to protect them. He didn't give you a choice," she said. "But I can. Look at them, Hal. Look how happy they are. They're free."

I scan the crowd of rotted humans swaying to the music and wearing grins that haven't graced a Dresden face in ages. They are sorrowing, sighing, bleeding, dying, and they're so serene as they stuff themselves with embryonic cream that I find myself leaning into the stone-cold tomb of Gloria's embrace.

## IT'S A WEIRD WINTER WONDERLAND

My lips part, and she pushes the donut inside. Every inch of my soul screams to spit it out, save one spot—and that's the place she prods. Closing her mouth on mine, she holds the sweetness in, tongues it down my throat, and fills the spot where the angels no longer sing. The devil's bitter perfume breathes a life of gathering gloom, and I sink into a grateful slumber as *Christmas Shoes* walks me into the dark.

# Liner Notes

Well, Happy Holidays, one and all.

*Santa-nic* cults, willful holiday manslaughter, murder, mayhem, armed robbery, sex, drugs, shapeshifting, and more sex.

That's what the holidays *should* be about. Don'tcha think?

When we came up with the idea for this book, it was a little more tame.

"Let's do a holiday crime collection!" I says to Mabel (in this case, Rob).

"Maybe we make it more inclusive, Christmas, Hanukkah, Kwanzaa..." Says he.

Nine months and a goodly number of emails later, and we had around twenty stories from some real solid writers. Badasses, rogues and villains, and a few real cutie-pies with demon eyes.

"We've got a problem." Says Rob (in other cases, Mabel), "This book doesn't make sense."

"How so?" Says I, reaching for more peyote and the remote control, with which to put on more new *Twin Peaks*.

"Half of these are weird, bizarro stuff..."

"Yeah, baby!"

"And the other half are straight up dark crime."

# IT'S A WEIRD WINTER WONDERLAND

So, I pause the DVR.

"But that's what we do here! *Dark Crime and Weird Fiction*. Says so on the poster." I point behind me, very helpfully illustrating my point by directing his gaze to the banner on the wall.

"And there's twenty stories..."

"Yeah, baby!"

*Twin Peaks* awaits.

"Nobody will buy this ninety-pound brick of a book, Axel."

"I don't know, man." I says, brushing him off. "We'll make the font really small – like, 3pt."

"Then it's an illegible brick."

"We'll sell it with a magnifying glass! Added value!"

"It would already cost $39.95 per book without adding a magnifying glass."

"What if... you buy the book. You get half now, half emailed to you on Boxing Day?"

"What?"

"Shush. *Twin Peaks* is on. Hand me my riding crop and that bowl of nacho cheese Bugles."

"Whatever. We're just going to have to split it into two books."

"And the brick of cream cheese..."

"What?"

## IT'S A WEIRD WINTER WONDERLAND

"Hand me that brick of cream cheese. Audrey's going to dance."

And thus, two books were born.

Of which, the piece of weirdo magnificence you hold in your hands is part one.

How did it actually come together?

First, as always, we talked to Scotty.

Scott Phillips is one of our favourite writers, and probably my own most favouritest fellow nerd in all the world. Scott writes an incredible series of very funny books about a schlubby 70's working man vampire named Pete. He also writes short stories about a bumbling man-beast with lung problems named Boone Butters. Rob and I are both so enamoured with all of Scott's work that we pretty much invite him over to play whenever we're working on anything. Check out his incredible zombie western yarn in *TALL TALES OF THE WEIRD WEST* if'n you don't believe me. You should also check out his Patreon page, which is about the best thing going on the web. www.patreon.com/scott_s_phillips

Once Scotty was on board, we figured it might actually be something we could put together.

Scott recommended Steve Brewer, whom I knew only by reputation – and a fine reputation at that. Steve writes some fantastic crime books as well – specifically the *Bubba Mabry* and *Jack Nolan* books - and while he's not usually known for short stories in anthologies (though he has 30 published books. 30!) he blessed us with one hell of a tale. That poor ol' grandma with her grandkids coming any minute...

David James Keaton is somebody I've wanted to work with ever since I heard him reading from his book THE LAST PROJECTOR on the *CrimeWave* podcast a few years ago. Any writer who can make me spit eggnog out my nose while describing a porn director having a mental breakdown, is somebody I want to know. DJK does not disappoint with his humorous, presumably-fictional account of a new-fangled way of communicating on the roadways.

Likewise, Will "The Thrill" Viharo is somebody I've had a writerly man-crush on for some time. Pulpy, retro, and way, way out there, man. Dig it. Will loves the things I love: Twin Peaks; B-movies; 50's sci-fi; Old Hollywood glam; a nice fez. Check out any of this man's work for a seriously hard-boiled pulp throwback to the good ol' days of sin and depravity, *Hollywood Babylon* style. I was you, I'd start with the *Vic Valentine P.I.* books.

## IT'S A WEIRD WINTER WONDERLAND

Not everybody was a stranger going into this. Not everybody was so far-flung as all of these American compeers. Some of our writers are from a lot closer to home (for *us*, not necessarily for you, *obviously*.)

Brent Nichols is a damn fine sci-fi writer, a tall, dark and handsome fella, with a voice that makes all the ladies swoon (sometimes in fear for their lives, sure, but only *sometimes*). Brent had a story about a sex robot with a superhero complex in our book AB NEGATIVE. I also once read a story he'd written about a guy getting involved in sex party shenanigans under a table at a Denny's, during a job interview... and it was the funniest damn thing I'd read in a long damn time. When he offered up his take on a Dickens classic, and explained that it involved prostitution and drug trade, and that he was calling it *Ho Ho Ho*? Yeah. Here's your money, Brent.

Sarah L. Johnson is a local gal. She works at the bookstore that we do most of our events in our little hometown of Cowtown. She is intelligent, composed, some say elegant... and she's surprisingly twisted. Her first short story collection, *SUICIDE STITCH* blew me away. Her story here – *Riven* - a teasing, come-hither

## IT'S A WEIRD WINTER WONDERLAND

invitation to join the devilish blood cult of Christmas Cool – was one of the main reasons that we decided to make two holiday books, and focus one on the weird stuff. Her equally twisted, morally complicated, and thoroughly epic first novel, INFRACTUS also landed in Poe's inbox, and we couldn't be happier. Look for that bad mammajamma soon!

Laurie Z. Little Laurie Zottmann. The wild card. The cutie-pie angel with the devil in her smile. Who knew? Laurie writes an endlessly entertaining blog called *Dark Little Critter*, wherein she works out her issues with the help of her imaginary raccoon friend, who is seemingly obsessed with human sexuality. Laurie is an accomplished freelance writer, frequently writes articles on parenting and mental health, and has several times destroyed all of the competition at open mic nights with her tales of ribaldry. In fact, she is the current Noir at the Bar champion of Calgary, Alberta. Her collection/memoir DARK LITTLE THERAPIST is coming viddy soon to blow your minds.

Finally, but always first in our hearts, and our TBR piles – Jessica McHugh – the Queen of Bizarre, the future Grand Dame of fiction. Mark my words. In a hundred years, when you, me, and this book

## IT'S A WEIRD WINTER WONDERLAND

are all dust, McHugh's statues will stand tall, pen-in-hand, cat-a-shouldered, reminding our great-grand-children to be the best badasses they can be. Jess is a force of nature. She's published something like 20 books in the time I've known her. She doesn't stop, and she doesn't slow down. She's written everything from Steampunk to tween books, and all points in-be-tween (Sorry. Lousy publisher humour.) Her horror is among the best in the biz. Her bizarre stuff is so far beyond, and so far out there, that she almost has her own genre. Jess was featured in the very first Coffin Hop Press book, *DEATH BY-DRIVE-IN*, all the way back in 2012, and nothing could make me happier than being able to include her here. You want weird? YOU GOT IT!

When Rob Bose and I got together to overhaul CHP and put things into high gear, one of the first projects on the list was this idea of a weird/crime holiday book. And while (like most things in publishing), it didn't follow the plan we originally laid out, we're pretty happy with the result. Not only do we get to unleash this beautiful monster on the world, all decked out in it's superb finery (by legendary artist extraordinaire Tom Bagley), but now we get to do it all again next holiday

# IT'S A WEIRD WINTER WONDERLAND

season with a book of crime stories that will curl your toes and steal your stockings. Keep an eye out for the companion volume *BABY, IT'S COLD OUTSIDE*, featuring some of the best crime writers this side of the planet has to offer.

Let me just finish up here. I'm out of cream cheese and Bugles. Coop is back on the case.

I want to give a huge shout-out to all of these amazing talents that have let us borrow their words. It wouldn't be the holidays without songs to sing and tales to tell, and you all knocked it all the way to the North Pole.

Tom Bagley, you magnificent bastard, thanks for putting a face on our marauding mistletoe monster. I can't imagine anybody else getting the magic and the madness the way you do.

And finally,

Rob?

Thanks for everything.

I'd still be sitting on the couch, covered in smear and cornmeal dust, if it wasn't for you kicking my ass and making things happen.

You're the Santa to my Claus.

Oh, and Poe's cage needs to be cleaned.

That's on *your* list, right?

## IT'S A WEIRD WINTER WONDERLAND

Axel Howerton
Publisher, editor, debauched idiot
Calgary, Alberta
October 2018

## IT'S A WEIRD WINTER WONDERLAND

## IT'S A WEIRD WINTER WONDERLAND

# About the Authors

STEVE BREWER
## Up the Chimney

Steve Brewer is the author of 28 books about crooks, including the Bubba Mabry mysteries and the recent Jackie Nolan thrillers *SHOTGUN BOOGIE* and *HOMESICK BLUES*. A former journalist, Brewer teaches in the Honors College at the University of New Mexico in Albuquerque.

DAVID JAMES KEATON
## Wreckless Eyeballing

David James Keaton's short fiction has appeared in over 50 publications, and his first collection, *FISH BITES COP! Stories to Bash Authorities* (2013) was named the 2013 Short Story Collection of the Year by **This Is Horror**. He also teaches composition and creative writing at Santa Clara University in California.

## IT'S A WEIRD WINTER WONDERLAND

LAURIE ZOTTMANN
## Saint Nikki's Revenge

Laurie Zottmann writes about the anger that lays on top of everything. She likes raccoons and pelicans, and wants everyone to admit what they're really thinking. Her favourite smells are coffee, hot wings, and the spray from tearing orange peels. Her memoir, *DARK LITTLE THERAPIST*, debuts in 2017

WILL "THE THRILL" VIHARO
## That's a Wrap

Will "the Thrill" Viharo is a freelance writer, pulp fiction author, B-movie impresario and lounge lizard at large. His published bibliography includes the retrospective anthology series *The Thrillville Pulp Fiction Collection* featuring all of his standalone novels, as well as the definitive omnibus *The Vic Valentine Classic Case Files* (both available from Thrillville Press). Gutter Books offers the first and final Vic Valentine novels, respectively, *LOVE STORIES ARE TOO VIOLENT FOR ME* and *HARD-BOILED HEART*. Additionally, Will has written two sci-fi collaborations with Scott

Fulks, *IT CAME FROM HANGAR 18* and *THE SPACE NEEDLER'S INTERGALACTIC BAR GUIDE*. For more info visit **www.thrillville.net**

SCOTT S. PHILLIPS
## A Vampire, a Burglar, and an Aging Hippie Walk into a Mall

Scott S. Phillips has written all kinds of stuff: films, TV, books, comics and even dialogue for talking dolls. He's the author of the *PETE, DRINKER OF BLOOD* series, as well as several other books. Scott wrote the screenplay for the cult action flick *DRIVE* (1997), and twelve episodes of the CW Network's *KAMEN RIDER DRAGON KNIGHT*.

Perhaps most importantly, he once performed as stand-in for the legendary Lemmy in the video for Motorhead's *"Sacrifice."*

SARAH L. JOHNSON
## Riven

Sarah L. Johnson lives in Calgary with her noisy family and two slightly bewildered cats. She wrangles literary events at an indie bookstore for money, runs ultra-marathons for fun, has a filthy mouth, and does daily battle with curly hair. Her short stories have appeared in Room Magazine, Plenitude Magazine, the Bram Stoker nominated *DARK VISIONS 1*, and *YEAR'S BEST HARDCORE HORROR VOLUME 2*. Her short story collection *SUICIDE STITCH* was released in 2016, and her debut novel *INFRACTUS* is available from Coffin Hop Press.

BRENT NICHOLS
## Ho Ho Ho

Brent Nichols is a raconteur, a sciolist, and a riant luftmensch. He writes science fiction, fantasy, and crime fiction, and mostly avoids the burdens of traditional employment. He's got a couple of novels with Bundoran Press, and short stories in several anthologies including *AB NEGATIVE* from Coffin Hop Press.

JESSICA MCHUGH
## Of Gathering Gloom

Jessica McHugh is a novelist and internationally produced playwright running amok in the fields of horror, sci-fi, young adult, and wherever else her peculiar mind leads. She's had twenty-one books published in nine years, including her bizarro romp, *THE GREEN KANGAROOS*; the best-selling *RABBITS IN THE GARDEN*; and her YA series, *THE DARLA DECKER DIARIES.*

### ROBERT BOSE (*Editor*)

Robert Bose has a fondness for the supernatural, bumbling criminals, and fine whiskey, not necessarily in that order. He's the editor of several upcoming books for Coffin Hop Press, and the author of myriad short stories including the recently published collection, *FISHING WITH THE DEVIL*. When not writing and editing, he's working on a grand design to take over the good parts of the Universe.

### AXEL HOWERTON (*Editor*)

Axel Howerton is the editor of several books, including the Arthur Ellis Award nominated *AB NEGATIVE*. He teaches at the Alexandra Writers Centre in Calgary, Alberta, and is the author of innumerable short stories and several novels spanning (and *smish-smashing*) genres from Crime to Urban Fantasy, including the hard-boiled detective caper *HOT SINATRA*, the modern gothic

## IT'S A WEIRD WINTER WONDERLAND

fairytale *FURR*, and the noir fable *CON MORTE*. *WOLF & DEVIL* series.

VISIT US ONLINE AT

WWW.COFFINHOP.COM

Made in the USA
Columbia, SC
03 April 2018